THE YULETIDE ANGEL

By Sandra Ardoin

PRAISE FOR *THE YULETIDE ANGEL*

What a delightful story! Sandra Ardoin mixes a healthy serving of intriguing characters with a dash of mystery to create a love story that's as sweet as the cakes her heroine bakes. Pour yourself a cup of hot cocoa, mulled cider or your favorite holiday beverage and treat yourself to *The Yuletide Angel*. You'll be glad you did.

~**Amanda Cabot**
Author of *The Christmas Star Bride*

In an era where society denied women the right to vote and forced them to depend upon their fathers and brothers for sustenance, one woman finds the courage to defy convention. Sandra Ardoin has done a wonderful job in her portrayal of Violet, the Yuletide Angel. Violet not only rises above societal restrictions but also conquers her own timidity through self-sacrifice and determination. Along the way, she finds unexpected romance. The Yuletide Angel is a perfect Christmas story. Nostalgic in scope, it also drives home a deeper spiritual truth to be found in charity—to be given for God's glory, rather than our vanity. Sandy weaves a great story and tells it well.

~**Linda Wood Rondeau**
Author of *A Christmas Prayer* and *It Really IS a Wonderful Life*

Rarely has a novella captivated me as quickly and as thoroughly as Sandra Ardoin's *The Yuletide Angel*. Her characters are endearing and the writing superb. I look forward to more stories from this talented author!

~**Myra Johnson**
Award-winning author of *When the Clouds Roll By*

The Yuletide Angel is a Christmas tale of love and hope that will warm your heart long after the tinsel is packed away. Well done, Sandra Ardoin!

~**Mary Ellis**
Author of *The Lady and the Officer*

THE YULETIDE ANGEL BY SANDRA ARDOIN
Published by Heritage Beacon Fiction
an imprint of Lighthouse Publishing of the Carolinas
2333 Barton Oaks Dr., Raleigh, NC, 27614

ISBN: 978-1941103890
Copyright © 2014 by Sandra Ardoin
Cover design by writelydesigned.com
Interior design by Reality Premedia Services Pvt. Ltd.
www.realitypremedia.com

Available in print from your local bookstore, online, or from the
publisher at: http://heritagebeaconfiction.com/

For more information on this book and the author visit:
http://sandraardoin.com

Brought to you by the creative team at Heritage Beacon
Susan Craft, Ann Tatlock, Brian Cross, Eddie Jones, Rowena Kuo, and
Meaghan Burnett.

Library of Congress Cataloging-in-Publication Data
Ardoin, Sandra.
The Yuletide Angel / Sandra Ardoin 1st ed.

Printed in the United States of America

Acknowledgments

Thank you, God, for allowing me the opportunity to go through this experience in Your time. Your ways and Your thoughts are higher than mine. (Isaiah 55:8)

Over the years, I've learned that writing is not a solitary profession. It takes a team. That team begins at home, and the members eventually spread like ripples on water. So a simple, but heartfelt, "Thank You" goes to …

My husband, Terry, and daughter, Catherine, for the patience they show when they want to say something and I shush! them until I've punched a few more keys.

My mother-in-law, Oraine Ardoin, for all her prayers. She never gave up.

Diana Flegal of Hartline Literary Agency for her belief in my ability and her hard work on my behalf.

Ann Tatlock, Susan Craft, and everyone else at Lighthouse Publishing of the Carolinas who have been involved in the acquisition, preparation, and marketing of this novella.

My critique partners, Heidi Chiavaroli, Phyllis Keels, and Nicole Miller—along with the many other writer friends I've made on this journey. They've provided their insight, wisdom, and encouragement each step of the way.

Every historical novelist willing to share their research into the time period in which I write. Their knowledge has been invaluable.

And to readers of *The Yuletide Angel*, I hope you love Hugh and Violet as much as I do. (Yes, writers do fall in love with their characters.)

CHAPTER ONE

December 1890

Hugh Barnes hid behind the winter skeleton of an oak tree near the rundown house on Kelsey Street and watched a shadowy figure creep up the porch steps. By the dull beam of the cloud-covered moon, he distinguished more movement than features. He needed no light to discern who skulked outside the widow's clapboard house. According to local accounts, he was witnessing a visit by The Yuletide Angel.

After opening the front door and leaving a flour sack bulging with good will, the angel tiptoed away. At the road, she turned and swept back toward town, her dark skirts swaying with her quick, bold steps.

Hugh blew a warm breath on his cold hands and stepped out from behind the tree. He kept his distance, but made certain the town's Christmas-season Samaritan remained in sight as she delivered food to someone else in need. He frowned as the crisp, December air bit his face. A bout of insomnia had led him to his bedroom window in time to see her leave her home well after midnight. Curiosity caused him to follow.

Violet Madison, his shy neighbor, was The Yuletide

Angel. He could scarcely take it in. What a beautiful woman! Perhaps not in the conventional, physical sense. However, she was not unattractive. Her black hair glimmered in sunlight despite being pinned into a tight ball at the nape of her neck. Her full and genuine smile, something she displayed too seldom, never failed to lift his spirits and change her countenance from sullen to striking. But, no, her greatest asset was not physical. She possessed a beautiful heart.

And a reckless streak.

Didn't she realize the risk she took by wandering the streets alone in the middle of the night? If he could follow her unseen, so could someone with an evil intent. What prevented one of the drunken sots at the tavern from accosting her—someone with his brother's character?

Fortunately, the last he'd heard, Kit lived in Pittsburgh, over a hundred miles north. Not so far it was likely Hugh would never see him again, but far enough to make it difficult for his ne'er-do-well brother to betray him a second time.

Following Violet in secret meant dodging between large trees and evergreens and ducking around sheds and the corners of houses. He never imagined he'd creep across the lawns of his friends and neighbors in the frosty darkness to protect a woman who insisted her deeds remain anonymous.

Not long ago, he and Violet had talked about The Yuletide Angel. In her soft and timid manner, she insisted the person went to great lengths to safeguard *his* identity. She even quoted the words of Jesus when He urged His followers not to let the left hand know what the right was doing lest they lose their reward.

Hugh's grunt sounded hollow in the night air. *How dense of me not to have guessed the truth.*

For the past hour, Violet had taken the Savior's warning to extremes. She should be safe and warm in her own home, not wandering around in the dark, tempting danger in a way that tripled his heartbeat.

Finally, Violet entered the front gate of the home she shared with her brother, and Hugh breathed easier. When she twisted to glance in all directions, he hid behind a shed and waited for her to slip inside her house.

Hugh stuffed his hands in his coat pockets and entered his own home next door. As far as he was aware, only he knew the identity of the person they called The Yuletide Angel.

For now, it would remain his secret.

***

Violet edged forward on the parlor chair and glanced at the stately woman standing at her brother's side. She lowered her chin. "Isn't your decision to marry rather sudden, Charles?"

"Sudden? Not at all. Lila agreed to wait a proper time for us to mourn Papa's death. That time has passed."

Violet pulled at the tatted lace border of the

handkerchief in her hand until it ripped away from the cotton square. "It's only been eight months."

While Violet extended the outer sign of mourning past its requirement, Charles had waited only as long as the barest propriety dictated to abandon the somber attire and armband. Who could blame him? Why should he live a life of mourning the dead when he had a lively and colorful flower such as Lila?

Her brother reached down and clasped her hands in his. "It's time we get on with our lives. Be happy for us, Violet."

"Certainly, I'm ..." The words stuck in her throat, too big to move past the swollen emotions. She gulped and forced the corners of her lips to rise. "I'm happy for you both."

What about her? What life did she have to get on with? She was twenty-seven and with no prospects. Why hadn't Papa accepted the truth and provided for her? No man of her acquaintance wanted a shy and unappealing spinster-in-the-making with little more to her name than a small, monthly allowance.

The face of Hugh Barnes, the grocer from next door, flashed in her mind. Laugh lines curved at the corners of his mouth and etched the skin around his indigo eyes. His friendliness and humor lit any room he graced.

If only ...

Yes, they had forged a friendship Violet treasured, but why should a handsome man consider marriage to a dowdy woman like her? Besides, Mr. Barnes made no secret of his commitment to remaining a bachelor.

"It will be the three of us living here. Nothing needs to change, dear." Lila spoke in a placating tone, as if reassuring a child, even though she was a good five years younger.

Violet freed her hands from her brother's hold. "Thank you." She might as well get used to saying those words.

Lila gazed at her beau. "Marriage to Charles will be the best Christmas gift I have ever received."

Christmas? Violet twisted the handkerchief into a knot. "You intend to marry at Christmastime?"

"On the twentieth." Lila leaned into Charles as he wrapped an arm around her shoulders. "We want to spend the holiday as man and wife."

"That's not even three weeks. Are you sure it allows enough time to make arrangements?"

"This woman is a wonder." Charles—the smitten ninny—grinned at his beloved. "We'll marry here, right in this room."

Violet glanced around the parlor. Though she had come to think of it as hers, it belonged to Charles. With the exception of the piano, the chair in which she sat, and a few mementos, the whole house belonged to Charles. Soon, Lila would lay claim to it too.

Violet rose from her seat. "There's so much to do and, apparently, little time."

Lila shook her head. "Please don't go to any trouble. It will be a simple ceremony."

 5

"She's already arranged everything. There's nothing for you to do." Charles patted Violet's back.

Her spine stiffened. He didn't need her now or in the future.

"There is one thing." Lila turned to Violet. "Will you be so kind as to make the wedding cake? I so enjoy your baking."

The compliment took her aback. She'd had no idea her future sister-in-law paid a whit of thought to the desserts she'd made. "Of course. Berta has the day off, so if you'll excuse me, I'll bring tea." She scuttled toward the hall, her footsteps light and her heart heavy.

In the kitchen, Violet set the kettle on the stove lid and covered her face with her hands. Would she become like a faithful mutt, tolerated and occasionally patted on the head—or back? And what about when children began to arrive, and space was needed? How long would it be before Charles asked her leave? Where would she go and how would she fend for herself on the meager amount she received each month? And what about the charity that gave her such pleasure?

She sighed and lowered her hands. While preparing the tea and arranging ginger cookies on plates, she mulled over Lila's request. It wasn't the first compliment she had received on her baking ability. The heads of various committees at church and around town regularly appealed to her to contribute cakes or pies for their fundraisers, and they sold well.

Violet's heart rate sped. Was it possible to supplement

her allowance, thereby supporting herself by selling bakery items? She backed up to the kitchen counter and crossed her arms. For years, she had dreamed of owning such a business, but never dared mention it to anyone. The world was almost one full year into the decade of the 1890s. Better opportunities for women existed, but few in Meadowmead owned businesses, and certainly no one in the circles in which the Madisons traveled.

Reality set in, bearing down on her shoulders like a boulder. Opening a bakery meant renting a storefront and purchasing equipment. Charles would never approve of her idea, nor would he provide the funds to help her. Add to her predicament her pathetic skills in dealing with people. How silly of her to entertain the thought. She placed the tea items on a large tray and carried them down the hall.

"Charles, I believe this room would look more open and cheerful with the sofa nearer the window and the wallpaper changed to something brighter. Don't you?"

Lila's words jerked Violet to a stop outside the room, rattling the cups and saucers.

"Whatever you want, darling."

Already, her brother's fiancée planned changes to the Madison home. Regardless of Lila's earlier proclamation, what did she have in mind for Violet?

She had heard a story once of a spinster faced with a similar circumstance. Eventually, the wife grew tired of having the woman underfoot and gave her husband an ultimatum. The penniless spinster soon found herself living in a room above a storefront and eating scraps from a nearby restaurant.

Though her offerings for the unfortunate were given year-round, Violet believed God had used the woman's story to spark the anonymous Christmastime forays last year. He had given her a calling—a purpose that she'd carried into this season.

Wouldn't it be ironic if The Yuletide Angel found *herself* in need of charity?

CHAPTER TWO

Hugh stocked tins of tomatoes on a shelf, one minute attentive to his job, the next focused on the front of the store. The bell over the door jangled. He jumped up and swung around to view the entrance. The woman was not Violet. His stomach sank for the fifth time in the past hour.

After his latest customer left, he opened his pocket watch. Two-forty. He snapped it shut. She should have been here by now. Every Tuesday since he opened H. C. Barnes' Grocery six months ago, Violet walked through that door at two o'clock with her basket in hand and a guarded smile on her face. Every Tuesday, he dropped whatever task he was doing to converse with her.

While many men sought a woman with little more than a pretty face, Hugh preferred one with a sharp mind, and Violet's intelligence surpassed most women he'd known. Happily for him, other men in town had not made the effort to become acquainted with it.

He bent between the display of canned tomatoes and cracker tins to peer out the front window. Where was she? He longed to see the gentleness in her expression and hear the sweetness of her voice. Frustrated, he shoved a stack of flour bags too hard. He grabbed them before they toppled.

Sharp as Violet may be, she showed poor judgment with her midnight excursions. Even so, discovering her generosity to those less fortunate had swelled his growing affection for her.

Should he ask permission to court her? He grinned. Wouldn't a courtship between them set tongues wagging?

From his first day in Meadowmead, he'd discouraged marriage-minded females and their mothers from considering him a target. Even if he were a simple grocer these days, word had gotten around of the sizeable bank account he'd amassed over the past ten years. In his estimation, success rather than personality tended to catch a woman's interest.

Several teasing conversations informed him they also considered him a handsome catch. He saw those women as silly and vain, too similar in character to both his mother and the woman to whom he'd once professed his love. He wouldn't make the same mistake twice.

Hugh grabbed a broomstick from behind the counter and walked out the front door. With more attention paid to his business rather than his personal life, he might discover the shoplifter who had stolen several items from the shelves in the past weeks.

He swept back and forth along the same spot while scanning Main Street. Two- and three-story, brick buildings ran for three-and-a-half blocks and edged side streets for another block. His grocery occupied a large space on the east side, dead center, and across from Wood Brothers Mercantile. People bundled in coats hastened along the walkways and darted in and out of the shoe store, butcher, millinery, and other businesses that served the growing town. He saw no sign of Violet in either direction.

A breeze whipped down his neck, and he shivered. It was too cold to remain outside without his coat. As he lifted the broom to walk back inside the store, Violet turned the corner a block away wearing the stark black coat and black hat that were her cold-weather standard. Her chin was pointed down, as usual. How she kept from running into someone, he couldn't fathom. Only last Wednesday night did she prowl the streets holding her head high.

Hugh marched with lengthy strides into the store and replaced the broom behind the counter, then pretended to tally the figures in his ledger.

When the bell tinkled, he looked up. "Good afternoon, Miss Madison."

She kneaded her gloved hands. A basket swung at her side. "Mr. Barnes."

"Why don't you stand by the stove until you're warm?"

For several silent minutes, she stood in the center of the room where the heat from the cast iron stove spread throughout a large portion of the store. The wood in its belly crackled, underscoring the silence between them.

Concern for Violet refused to leave him—he always thought of her as Violet instead of Miss Madison. Tomorrow being Wednesday, The Yuletide Angel was scheduled to make another round. He wouldn't stop her, but she wouldn't go alone.

So far she had experienced safe travels. Nonetheless, if she continued her charitable missions through Christmas Eve, as he'd heard happened last year, she did so at great risk to her welfare. Her reputation might suffer. Her very life might be lost.

He shut the ledger. "Better?"

The velvet hat she wore covered much of her head but couldn't hide her drawn mouth and the slight shadows under her eyes. "Yes. Thank you."

Hugh bent, planted his elbows on the counter, and crossed his arms. "I took your advice and read *A Connecticut Yankee in King Arthur's Court.*"

Her full, rosy lips spread with unmistakable pleasure. "You liked it?"

"I did." He paused. "Tell me, Miss Madison, if it were possible to go back in time, where would you go?"

Without a second beat, she said, "I would captain a sailing ship in the early part of the century … a schooner, I think."

Captain a schooner? "Astounding. Have you ever sailed?"

"Not once."

"Then why?"

 12

She resettled the basket dangling from her arm and looked away as if trying to hide the hint of additional pleasure. "For the adventure, Mr. Barnes."

He laughed. "You are a daring woman, Miss Madison."

The bell jingled. Mrs. Julian, a robust woman of infinite words, burst into the store and shattered their moments of candor. "My, it's a good day for soup and hot coffee, wouldn't you say so, Mr. Barnes?" Before he could answer, she pranced toward Violet, who shrank back until she bumped into the stove and leapt forward again. The older woman plowed on. "I heard the news of the engagement, Miss Madison. We're all thrilled. I'm sure you are, too."

Hugh stiffened. Violet was getting married? To whom? He'd never seen her with anyone, never heard news that a man courted her. The hope in his heart sank like a stone.

"Lila Blackstone is a lovely woman. She'll make your brother the perfect wife."

Hugh released a pent-up breath. Ah, Charles was marrying Miss Blackstone. He should have realized.

"He's very happy, Mrs. Julian." Violet stepped past the woman and inspected the onions filling a nearby crate, apparently finished with the subject of her brother's engagement.

Perhaps his help would hurry the woman on her way. "Is there something I can get for you, Mrs. Julian?"

He spent the next few minutes gathering items from

around the store and recording them in the ledger on the counter while listening to the woman drone on about one insignificant topic or another. Once she left, he turned to Violet. "I didn't realize—"

She held up a gloved hand. "Please don't. I wish to hear no mention of marriage."

He blinked several times as if the action would remove his bewilderment. Had she no desire to court anyone, including him?

***

Mr. Barnes walked around the grocery counter as if he suspected a physical attack from her; something far from Violet's mind, but not impossible given her current mood.

She was happy for Charles. Really. He should be married, and once she and Lila became better acquainted, Violet hoped they would get along. Both being their parents' sole daughter provided them with something in common. In time, they might even grow as close as true sisters.

But the congratulations of others had been ceaseless over the past few days, and each one brought with it a reminder of the state of her own life. In pondering her situation since last Friday, she had prayed for an answer to the uncertainty and had been led time after time to the idea of selling bakery items.

Since she had no funds for a storefront, Violet had thought of an alternative, something to get her toes wet

 14

without drowning her in debt. Thus far, she had met failure. Though she had not wanted to take advantage of their relationship, her grocer friend was her last chance.

"I'm sorry, Mr. Barnes. I'd rather discuss something else if you don't mind."

"What is it, Miss Madison?"

Violet ran her tongue across her bottom lip, caught it between her teeth, and promptly let it loose. Her lips were already rough from the cold. She needn't increase their ugliness. If she ever hoped to support herself, she must shake off the "Shrinking Violet" label from her school days and become a woman of poise and determination.

She set the basket and its contents on the counter. Despite her best intention, her fingers trembled as she folded back the edges of the napkin covering a small spice cake. He peeked inside and inhaled. Seeing his anticipation warmed her as the stove in his store had no power to do.

"For me?"

Violet removed the cake and set it on the counter next to the basket. "Will you taste it? I would like your opinion."

"All right, but I warn you, I'm an expert when it comes to sweets." He pinched off a chunk of cake, releasing the scents of cinnamon, nutmeg, and cloves, and popped the raisin-filled morsel in his mouth. He closed his eyes and rewarded her with a sigh of bliss. A good sign, but one she'd seen twice today. Neither time brought her closer to her goal.

 15

"Well?"

Mr. Barnes swallowed. "Delicious. You're an exceptional baker, Miss Madison."

"Thank you." His reaction sent a quiver of delight through her, more so than the compliments of the other merchants. But her purpose was not personal. It was business. She must not confuse the two or allow him to do so. "I hoped you'd think so because after I've tested my ability to sell my desserts, I plan to open a bakery."

His brows shot toward the tin ceiling. "A bakery?"

"Is that so shocking?" At least he hadn't laughed at her like the others ... not yet.

"A bit, but I must say you're a woman of many surprises. Many good surprises."

Another thrill rushed through her veins. "Then I have a ... a favor to ask."

"What is it?" Unlike the other gentlemen she'd approached, his expression showed no sign of wariness.

"Will you consider adding a few of my cakes and pastries to your store?" She hurried the question as she trotted to a corner near the back of the room. "I'll bring a table and place it here. It will be out of the way of your other merchandise. Of course, I would share any profits with you. Would twenty-five percent be satisfactory? Or perhaps you would prefer I rent the—"

"Stop, Miss Madison."

Violet's mouth snapped shut. She trudged back to the counter and picked up the basket. "I'm sorry. I have

16

no desire to take advantage of our ... of our acquaintance, Mr. Barnes. Please forget I asked." She started for the door.

"Miss Madison ... Violet. I'm not upset that you asked." He met her in the center of the store.

"But you can't help me."

"May I give you a word of advice?"

She nodded.

"You won't go far in business with a defeated attitude."

When he proceeded toward the door, Violet prepared to be shown out of the store. At the last second, he angled right and stopped in front of the large display window. "This will prove a more appropriate place, visible to those outside and easy to find."

She gasped. Had she heard correctly? Was her dream about to come true? "Then you agree?"

"It will be my privilege to provide you a trial period in which to test your abilities, though I doubt they need testing. Be that as it may, I recommend you start small before risking too much investment."

The caution kindled an urge to tease the sober words away. "You advised me to be optimistic, Mr. Barnes."

"Optimistic, not rash."

She held out her hand. "Thank you."

He took her hand, but rather than shake it, he gave it the gentlest squeeze and retained it longer than necessary or proper. Even through the kid leather of her gloves, his strong fingers warmed hers. When combined with his intense scrutiny, she wasn't sure her nerves would survive the contact.

Only then did it occur to Violet that he'd called her by her Christian name.

CHAPTER THREE

In the middle of the night on Wednesday, more accurately Thursday morning, Violet stopped by the side of the road and tucked the collar of her coat closer to her neck. She shivered down to her toes. The worst part of her calling was walking in the bone-chilling, late-night cold. If it were daylight, and these weren't secret missions of mercy, she would use the horse and carriage Charles kept in the barn behind the house.

No matter. She would not allow the temperature to deter her from providing someone a needed meal. The gift wasn't much, but she could endure this weather for an hour or two once a week to know it was received with joy. And the newspaper or local gossip mill always indicated the recipient's joy, which in turn brought happiness to Violet.

She lugged three heavy flour sacks containing canned goods, staples, and homemade bread and used the feeble light from the quarter moon to guide her to her first stop, the tiny cottage of an elderly woman. Since the death of her son earlier in the year, the poor lady worked hard to fill her pantry. No one in Meadowmead locked up at night, so Violet opened the front door with care and set one of the sacks inside. Then she made her way to the next stop one block over, the home of a blind man. At this house, she tied the sack to the door so he wouldn't miss it.

At her third stop, she approached the front porch of a young man raising his niece and nephew. Violet had not met the family but had heard of them through Charles. Her brother never spoke well of the uncle, claiming he had too great a taste for spirits. While she lauded the man's willingness to raise the orphaned children, his penchant for alcohol left them lacking in necessities.

Once more, she set the bag inside, closed the door, and turned to leave.

Crack! A twig snapped.

Violet froze. She slowly turned and peered into the surrounding blackness. Her heart pounded like a hammer trying to knock a hole in her chest.

She had never worried about traveling through town at this time of night. Who else would roam the streets other than her and those in the tavern? She made a point of keeping far from that place. Was it the uncle returning from a bout of drinking?

Leaning forward, she listened for other sounds. Nothing. As she crept away, her skin prickled with the sensation of being watched.

She picked up speed and arched her shoulders, prepared for something or someone to reach out and grab her. She dashed down the path along her street, through the front gate, and up to the door of her house. Panting with the exertion, she opened the screen and front doors, retaining the presence of mind not to let either of them slam and wake Charles.

She tiptoed to the window in the parlor and surveyed the landscape, likely a worthless effort in the dark, but ...

To get a better look, she pressed her nose to the cold glass, then with her coat sleeve, wiped away the fog from her breath. A shadow darted across the edge of Mr. Barnes' yard. Or was it her imagination?

Violet climbed the stairs and entered her room while praying for the courage to continue her charitable endeavor or the wisdom to lay it aside.

If the shadow belonged to someone who followed her, why hadn't she been accosted? The shiver that attacked her in the privacy of her room had nothing to do with the cold.

***

Once he reached his bedroom, Hugh whipped off his tie and unbuttoned his shirt in the dark. He ran a hand down his face and covered a yawn. He'd be glad when Christmas passed, and Violet gave up her late-night expeditions, not only for her sake, but for his. Lack of sleep made him grumpy, and a grumpy grocer did not bode well for business.

Hugh frowned at his dim reflection in the bureau mirror as he recalled Violet's swift trip home after the final delivery. Perhaps she merely raced the clock in an attempt to return before being found missing. Several times, though, she had glanced over her shoulder or stopped and cocked her head as if to listen. She'd almost caught him once. Had he frightened her?

Violet's alarm began after the last delivery. With little cover near the house, he had been forced to wait quite a distance away or risk discovery. Had something happened in the brief time she was out of his sight?

He'd ask to accompany her in the future, but he was sure she would not welcome his intrusion. As well, if they were caught prowling the streets at night together, it would ruin her. He'd gladly pass from one place of concealment to another to protect her from trouble caused by any late night mischief makers.

Hugh yanked back the sheet, climbed in bed, and dropped onto the pillow. Should he inform Charles of her activity, ruining any good opinion she had of him? No. He'd continue his secret pursuit to keep her safe. His chest constricted with the weight of his responsibility.

Her secret guardian. How would she react if she found out they were partners in more than business?

Violet planned to bring her first baked goods into the store in a few hours. He had sensed desperation in her desire to find a place to sell her goods. Why? What drove her to suddenly want to become a businesswoman? At least she had chosen his store over other possible merchants in town.

Hugh folded his hands under his head and studied

the ceiling. Today might be the right time to explore her feelings for him. If he asked the right questions, her answers would indicate whether or not she approved of a courtship between them.

He envisioned escorting her around town. On their way to supper at the hotel, her fingers would rest on his arm, and he would draw her close to whisper words meant only for the ears of the woman he courted. In spring, they'd stroll through the park and marvel at the beauty of newly-budded foliage and the sweet smell of roses and honeysuckle.

But what if she didn't approve? What if she meant what she'd said yesterday, that she had no desire to speak of marriage?

He turned on his side and mumbled a prayer for good sense where Miss Madison was concerned, then drifted into a deep sleep.

***

Violet set the plate filled with Berta's scrambled eggs and ham in front of Charles, who sat at the head of the dining room table. She took her seat on one side. For several minutes, she shuffled eggs around her plate and sought the words to tell her brother of her new venture.

She glanced at his half-eaten food. If she didn't say something soon, he'd be finished and ready to leave for his job at the bank. She set her fork down and wiped her hands on the napkin in her lap. "Charles, on your way to work, would you mind driving me to Mr. Barnes' store?"

He halted in the process of buttering another piece of toast to gape at her. "The grocer? I thought you did your shopping on Tuesday. And why so early? I doubt the store is open." The toast crunched as he bit into it.

She refused to let his skepticism chill her excitement, so she raised her chin in a deliberate display of mutiny. "I'm not shopping today, Charles. I'm delivering baked goods to Mr. Barnes."

"Baked goods? I thought I smelled …" He turned in his seat to glance at the door leading into the kitchen, then swiveled back around. "To Hugh Barnes? Is there something I should know about your relationship with our neighbor that would possess you to bake for him?"

Violet's lips parted, and heat rose to flood her neck and face at his insinuation, an insinuation she wished had merit. "My cakes and pies are not for Mr. Barnes to eat. They're to sell in his store."

Charles dropped the toast and jolted upright in his seat. His stare pierced her. "To sell?"

Though she quaked inside, she couldn't let it show. "Y-yes. If all goes well, I hope to rent a storefront and open a bakery in the near future."

"Have you taken leave of your senses? You want to become a merchant? A baker?" His head shook in an agitated manner reminiscent of their father's. "Absolutely not. I forbid it. I cannot believe Hugh Barnes agreed to this. He did agree? You're not planning to ambush him, are you?"

"Of course he agreed. In fact, he advised me of the proper procedures for m-my undertaking." Her voice quivered. "I am an adult, Charles. You can't forbid me and keep me from doing what is in my best interest. It isn't unheard of for a woman to work or own a business these days."

He leaned forward. "Your best interest? What is that supposed to mean?"

"You and Lila will be married soon."

"And?"

"Naturally, she'll want to run your household. There will be little room for me here, especially once your children arrive."

"Our chil … Do not set the cart to dragging the horse, Violet." The corner of his mouth convulsed with a tic. "Do you honestly believe I would turn you out on the street? You're my sister. You have no one else. It's my duty to take care of you."

She bristled. She shouldn't be, nor did she want to be, anyone's duty.

Charles attempted a grin, but it looked more like a grimace. "Violet, dear, your looks are pleasant enough. If you would make an effort to be more social, you would attract a fine gentleman to take care of you. It isn't too late."

A scream of frustration rose in her throat, but she swallowed it just in time. Notwithstanding his assurance of a home, he could not guarantee his bride would feel the same way in another six months or a year.

25

They agreed on one thing. She could no longer afford to be known as Shrinking Violet.

She stood, picked up her plate, and marched in the direction of the kitchen. "If you will not help me transport my goods to Mr. Barnes, I'll do it myself."

CHAPTER FOUR

Hugh pressed the tips of his fingers into the corners of his grainy eyes before moving across the store in measured steps. He'd barely unlocked the door before Violet arrived in her brother's carriage. The bell jangled, and she scuffled inside carrying a large basket and a book trapped under her arm. Like swift waters washing away debris, the sight of her swept away his fatigue.

"Let me, Miss Madison." He set her basket on the counter.

After breathing in the sweet aromas of sugar and apples, he made up his mind to be her first customer. It was fair, since he'd been her first choice in merchants.

"Your fresh cakes will attract customers like birds to bread crumbs." He pointed to the account book in her hand. "I see you brought your own ledger."

"To keep our sales separate. Is that all right? Will it be too much trouble?"

"Not at all." Nothing about having the pleasure of her company for a time each day would be too much trouble. If everything went well, they might work out a deal soon in which he'd buy her goods outright.

Charles entered the store carrying a rectangular

table, apparently removed from a room of the Madison home. "Where do you want this, Barnes?" The man spit out the words and aimed a scowl at his sister.

Hugh pointed to the vacant spot he'd cleared for her use. "In front of the window."

Charles dropped the table with such force Hugh expected the legs to break.

Violet winced and scurried to the door. "I'll get the other basket from the carriage."

Charles waited until his sister walked outside, then tugged on Hugh's sleeve and pulled him to the back of the store. "Why did you insert yourself into Violet's preposterous scheme?"

Hugh matched his lowered voice, but not the hiss. "She came to me with the idea, and I thought it a good one. Violet is a talented baker."

"That doesn't make her a businesswoman, Barnes. You know a successful merchant shows a competency for friendliness and salesmanship. Violet struggles to maintain the barest of conversations." Charles narrowed his eyes. "Be warned. I will mind my sister's accounts."

Hugh curled his fingers. "Are you insinuating that I'm a cheat? Because if you are, you should know that I agreed to a much smaller percentage of her sales than I would have for anyone else." His respect for Violet was all that kept him from tossing her brother onto the street.

A throat cleared behind him. When he turned, Violet pointed to the basket on the table. "I brought four cakes, three pies, and a dozen tarts. Do you think that's too many? If so, I'll send some to the bank with Charles."

It might be excessive for her first day, but Hugh refused to discourage her. It sounded like her brother did well enough in that area. Whatever remained at closing, he would buy—anything to prove Charles wrong. "It's a good start. Better to have too many than leave a customer wanting."

Her gaze flashed to her brother and settled on Hugh again. "I'll set everything out."

With her busy, Hugh turned back to Charles. "I understand your concern. Miss Madison may be inexperienced, but she's not incompetent. You can trust me to guide her. You have my word."

The starch never faded from the man's stance. "I'll hold you to it."

Clearly, Charles cared for his sister, or he wouldn't have attacked Hugh's motives. If the man knew of Violet's activities only a few hours ago and his part in that adventure, he would lay Hugh out on the planks under their feet. Right or wrong, he could not bring himself to betray Violet.

"Why did you make this agreement, Barnes? What do you have to gain?" Before Hugh could reply, he added, "She told me you were the only merchant who allowed her space for her goods. You should have turned her down like the others."

"The others?"

While Charles related Violet's appeals to his competition, the muscles across Hugh's back grew taut. She had not regarded him as her first choice after all. He had been her last resort.

***

"Thank you, Charles." Violet clasped her hands behind her back before she gave in to her inclination to push her brother and his dour attitude out the door. Whatever he and Mr. Barnes discussed—and she had no doubt it concerned her—it did nothing to improve his testy frame of mind.

Surely her brother had ruined her opportunity. Perhaps threatened her business benefactor? It was like Charles to treat her as though she needed protection from herself and everyone else—just as Father had done for years.

She waited by her display table for Mr. Barnes to tell her he'd changed his mind, and she should gather her things to follow Charles out the door. Instead, he bent over his ledger ignorant to the fact her every nerve was on edge.

As the seconds passed and he said nothing, she smoothed an oilcloth she'd brought from home over the tabletop and tugged this way and that to arrange it evenly. Not all her baked goods would fit on the table at once, so she set out samples on paper doilies she'd purchased at the mercantile. After adding one apple cake, one chocolate cake, an apple pie, and a half-dozen cherry tarts, she stepped back, pleased with the arrangement. She breathed in the sweet mixture of sugar, spices, and chocolate frosting. Now if the customers who stopped by the table found the display as pleasing and irresistible, she'd prove her ability and usefulness to her brother and, perhaps, her neighbor.

"Would you mind if I left the rest in the basket, Mr. Barnes? I'll come back this afternoon to see if there's a need to place more on the table."

"I'm confident there will be a need for more, Miss Madison." When he looked up from his ledger, those laugh lines deepened with his smile. "I hope you'll allow me first choice."

"I'm sorry." She yanked the towel covering off the basket. "I should have offered. Please take your pick, and I won't accept payment."

"Miss Madison …" His brow slanted as if he considered his next words carefully. "Since we are business associates now, may I call you Violet—in private, naturally?"

Was it proper? They had known one another for several months, and their relationship was branching out in a new direction. Why shouldn't they use Christian names … in private? "Yes, if I may I call you Hugh."

Oh, Violet, less than half an hour in business and look how bold you've become!

"I'd be honored." He opened the cash drawer on the register. "Let me see your list of prices."

She handed him the paper on which she'd written each item, along with the amount she hoped to charge.

 31

"I estimated the cost of all the ingredients and added your percentage, plus a small amount for my labor. The prices aren't too high, are they?"

He scanned the sheet. "They look fair. In fact, you might want to increase the price of the pies by a few pennies." He reached into his pocket, sorted through a handful of coins, and added several to the cash drawer. "Please make a note in your ledger that you've sold one apple cake."

Violet chose not to argue over the money and entered the information on the first line of the book. Her first sale! *Lord, please don't let it be the last.*

"You're very kind, Mr.—"

He cocked his head and waited.

"Hugh."

The corners of his mouth turned up. A few minutes later, Violet walked out the door with her head held high, seeing a whole new world before her.

***

On Monday, Violet carried a basket inside Hugh's store and set it next to the empty table. "Good morning … H-Hugh."

"Good morning." He stood behind the store counter, his chest quaking with an inner chuckle. She still stumbled over his given name on occasion, but there was something to be said for relaxing formalities. Since agreeing to do so, she had seemed more comfortable around him. Each time they met he discovered insights into the woman others passed off as uninteresting.

Who would have guessed she embraced the adventure of setting sail to parts unknown or wept at the words to the hymn, *Nearer My God to Thee*?

"It's a beautiful day for December, isn't it?"

"Yes, ma'am, it is. I figure we'll receive more snow in a day or two, though."

Rather than mope over the fact Violet had come to him last to sell her goods, he'd decided to appreciate that she chose him at all and be grateful the other merchants turned her down. His sales had risen and, on Saturday, he served two women he had lost to the only other grocer in town, a man who sold inferior but cheaper goods.

Hugh frowned at the book in front of him. His sales were up, but he persisted in dealing with a thief. What was he to do while one customer required his help, and another roamed the store, free to pick up and carry out whatever he wanted?

Violet started for the back room where he had kept the leftover pies and cakes from the day before.

"You won't find anything back there."

She stopped. "Why not?"

"Everything sold Saturday," he winked at her, "by two o'clock."

Her molasses-colored eyes widened. "Everything? Even the little tarts?"

"Yes. Mrs. Julian came in Friday afternoon. Evidently, the scalloped lattice-work on your pies is unique. She recognized your handiwork before seeing

 33

your name on the sign. With that woman around, you'll never need to advertise." He handed her a sheet of paper. "I took a couple of orders. I hope you don't mind."

Violet read the request for an apple cake and a dozen cherry tarts. "I don't mind. I only hope I can fill them to your customers' satisfaction."

"They're your customers now too." He moved around the counter to stand near her. "You'll be a success, Violet. Don't doubt yourself."

A soft pink colored her cheeks. "I'm grateful to you for your thoughtfulness. If you hadn't given me this opportunity, I'm not sure what I would have done. After Charles marries …" The statement dropped off as if the words fell over a cliff. She walked to the table near the window. "I brought six dozen oatmeal cookies. I'll add them to the price list. If they don't sell today, they'll be good tomorrow."

So her brother's marriage was the motivation behind her sudden plan to open a bakery. He should have known she would worry over her place in his household. The realization kindled a greater desire to protect her while seeing to it she felt worthy of esteem.

Hugh grabbed the newspaper he'd been reading before she came into the store and ambled over to the table. "There's another story in the Gazette about The Yuletide Angel's last deliveries. Have you seen it?"

Violet emptied the basket, her attention on the items she'd brought. The slight tremble of her fingers gave away her anxiety. "No. Charles has the paper delivered to the bank and reads it there. I rarely see it."

"The people of Meadowmead are fortunate to know such a compassionate person lives in their midst." He studied her face, which was as tight as a well-strung violin. "I wonder who we have to thank."

She halted in the midst of arranging her products. "As we've already discussed, I'm sure whoever it is, she … or he … does the deed without requiring a thank you. Otherwise, why would the person prefer to remain anonymous? We must honor that preference."

Hugh had given her the chance to admit to her good work, and she had not sought personal gratitude. What a beautiful and humble woman. He had never known anyone who sparked such esteem in him.

"That doesn't diminish my admiration for The Yuletide Angel, Violet. On the contrary, it heightens it."

That smile he loved so well brightened his day and chased away any lingering reservations about courting her.

CHAPTER FIVE

Pressing her lips together, Violet grappled to control the rebellious happiness that betrayed her. Hugh Barnes admired her.

Then the truth seeped in and her delight ground to an abrupt halt. He admired The Yuletide Angel, not Violet Madison. If she admitted her secret identity to him would he find her more attractive? Would he consider courting her?

The feather in her hat waved with the slight shake of her head. God had not given her the task of helping others in order to boast about it or use it to gain the interest of the man *she* admired more than any other. She held to the scripture in Matthew 6 that commanded she not sound a trumpet about her good deeds. Where was God's blessing in that?

And He had blessed her. He'd brought her customers who bought her baked goods, and He'd used Hugh Barnes to build her self-assurance. She peeked at him as he opened a crate of canned milk several feet away. Perhaps, one day, he would see her as more than his spinster neighbor or someone who prepared a tasty apple cake.

In the meantime, she would continue to bake each day, all day. Charles disapproved, but it made no difference. She'd purchased the ingredients with her allowance, so she hadn't plundered the household supplies. While the work interfered with her other tasks at home, she had never felt so alive, so energetic.

Cakes. Pies. Cookies.

She dropped the towel in the basket. Charles had chosen his future. Surely this was hers.

The door opened. A ragged man close to her age stepped inside trailed by two children. The boy, possibly nine or ten, was tall for his age. The girl appeared to be around seven. Adorable children, even with disheveled blond hair and dirty faces. Hugh's interest never wavered from the man as he walked around the store.

Violet laid the last of the cookies in a small box. If she wanted to prepare for tomorrow as well as fill the orders given to her, she must return home and start baking. With her chin tucked, she turned to go and ran into a wool-covered wall that reeked with a blend of wood smoke, cigar smoke, a woman's perfume, and sour alcohol. The stench nauseated her, more from the knowledge those poor children lived with such a shiftless sort than the physical attack to her senses.

Before the man could reach out to steady her, Hugh pushed between them. "Please watch where you're going, Mr. Collinsworth."

Collinsworth? The man for whom she'd left provisions last Wednesday? Violet glanced at the children, grateful to have supplied the sustenance; small as it was. The boy studied her as if she were an insect specimen. His blue stare intimidated her.

Hugh clasped her upper arms and set her back a step. Then he let her go. "Are you all right, Miss Madison?"

"Yes."

Hugh scowled at the man. Mr. Collinsworth hadn't even removed his hat in her presence, but she didn't want to cause her friend the loss of a customer when the accident was her fault. She opened her mouth to apologize for not watching where she was going.

"Weren't nothin' but an accident, Barnes." The two men sized each other up. Finally, Mr. Collinsworth removed his hat. "Sorry, ma'am."

"I'll see you tomorrow morning, Miss Madison." Hugh led the man away with the little girl following. "What can I get for you, sir?"

The two men conducted business and Violet picked up her basket to leave. The boy stood at the table with his back to her, ogling her baked goods. Business had been good these first days. She could afford to part with a few cookies. But, before she had the opportunity to voice the offer, he grabbed a handful and stuffed them in the pocket of his coat.

Though her mouth fell open, no words escaped. What should she say? Stealing was wrong, and that was the boy's intent.

He twisted and found her watching. His hand slipped into his pocket, and he shifted from one foot to another. Sweat broke out on his forehead. At least the child showed signs of remorse.

"What's your name?"

His small Adam's apple throbbed. "Mitch Collinsworth, ma'am. I didn't mean to take 'em."

He pulled the cookies halfway out of his pocket, and she stilled his hand with a firm hold. "Be sure to share them with your sister, Mitch."

"You mean you don't want 'em back?"

"What I want is a promise you'll never take what isn't yours in the future."

He glanced at his uncle and Hugh. "Yes, ma'am. Uh … no, ma'am. I won't."

Perhaps she should make another delivery to the Collinsworth home this week.

***

The next morning Violet raced around the kitchen, adding items to her basket with less care than normal. With her forearm, she pushed strands of unruly hair away from her eyes.

"If you insist on carrying on your irrational escapade, Violet, we must go." Charles clicked the pocket watch shut and stomped out of the kitchen.

He'd spent extra time at the breakfast table, attempting to talk her out of that "irrational escapade." Now, they both ran late.

She picked up the tray of cherry tarts and whipped around. Her petticoat tangled around her legs and she

 39

tripped as she stepped toward the basket. Tarts flew through the air like a flock of frightened black birds. She lunged to catch one or two, but they passed through her hands and smashed onto the floor with the others. The tray crashed alongside the broken mixture of shells and fruit.

Violet dropped to her knees. "No, no, no. Oh, no."

Her brother rushed into the room. "What happened? Did you fall?" He helped her up. "Are you hurt?"

"I'm fine." She stomped her foot. "Oh, for pity's sake!"

Both Berta and Charles gawked at her as if she had broken into that scandalous can-can dance right in the middle of the kitchen.

"Violet, you never lose your temper."

"Maybe I should on occasion, Charles."

He fisted his hands on his hips. "This proves what I was saying earlier. You do not have the temperament to be in business. Look how you've changed in less than a week's time."

She drew in a deep breath and counted to five, then added five more counts for good measure. "Charles, you had better leave without me or you'll be late for work. I have to fill the order I received, so I'll be busy most of the morning preparing more tarts to replace the ones I dropped."

"Violet—"

"Please stop and let Mr. Barnes know what happened and that I'll be in later. I don't want him to wonder if he'll receive the items I promised."

Charles huffed. "Since when did you become so stubborn and bossy?" He picked up the basket with the rest of her goods. "I'll take these with me."

"Thank you."

Once he left, she glared at the mess on the floor, then dropped to her hands and knees to help Berta clean every flake of crust and dollop of sticky fruit filling from the boards. Only on rare occasions did she lose her temper, and it always led to an apology and repentance, even if it was lost in a righteous anger. This time, she had not apologized. Not even a tiny bit of regret scolded her. Well, perhaps a smidgen.

Violet sat back on her heels. "Berta, do you think Charles is right? Have I changed?"

The housekeeper shrugged her shoulders. "You do appear more outgoing, Miss Violet."

"That's good, isn't it?"

"Forgive me if I speak out of place, but you also seem happier these days. Unless we count a few minutes ago." Berta cackled and threw a handful of broken tart crust into a bucket. "But it's good to see you stand up for yourself."

Less than an hour later, Violet slid a batch of new tarts into the oven and climbed the stairs to change her cherry and flour-splattered walking dress. After washing pink speckles from her face, she chose the new red wool, twill suit with the black, braided trim on the jacket and fitted, bone bodice. It had been a daring purchase—for her, anyway—but she was tired of the drab colors her father had insisted she wear. If she wanted Hugh Barnes to look at her as she'd seen other men look at women they found appealing, she must do something bold.

She smoothed the wool material and peered into the full-length mirror, pleased with the image. Almost.

Her hair stood out in all directions.

She removed the pins, brushed it until it shimmered, and re-pinned it to create a softer style. She hoped to match the one in a picture she'd seen in a recent issue of *Ladies Home Journal*. Violet compared her result with the drawing. Something wasn't right. She twisted a few strands of hair around the hot iron, which added wisps of curl at the edges of her face.

She peeked into the mirror and laughed. If she hadn't known the woman in the looking glass, she might have worked up the courage to introduce herself.

A horse whinnied in the street. Curious, she sashayed to the window and peered out. A man exited a closed carriage parked between the Madison and Barnes' houses. The stranger gazed at the front of Hugh's home. His shoulders rose and fell with a deep breath before he ventured up the walk.

Violet reached for the window to call out to him that her neighbor was not at home, but drew her hand back. She didn't know the visitor and didn't want to appear nosy. Besides, he'd discover it for himself soon enough. She walked out of the room and descended the stairs.

After donning a full apron and wrapping a towel around each hand, she pulled the tarts from the oven. Once they cooled, she would carry them to the store. She sighed at the delay. It wasn't thoughts of fresh air and a cold walk, or an order filled that set a quiver in her heart.

At the sudden *brrnnng* of the door bell, she almost dropped the second batch of tarts.

"I'll answer it, Berta." She set the metal sheet holding the hot little pies on her worktable, removed the apron, and strode to the foyer.

The gentleman she'd seen in front of Hugh's house stood on the other side of the screen door. Violet tried not to stare, but it was no use. If it was possible, he was more handsome than her neighbor with his strong chin and the sparkle in his icy blue eyes.

He removed his hat. "Good morning, ma'am. I stopped at the house next door, but no one is home."

With the satchel in his hand, she assumed he was a peddler, though his dignified posture and dapper attire didn't resemble any she had ever met. "I'm sorry, sir, I have no time to look through your wares this morning."

The man beamed, highlighting charming and familiar features that curled the toes in her shoes. "You misunderstand, ma'am. I'm looking for Mr. Barnes. I was told he lives over there." He pointed toward Hugh's house.

"Yes, but he'll be at the store at this hour. He owns a grocery in town."

"My name is Christopher Barnes. Hugh is my brother."

"I didn't know he had a brother." Violet curled her fingers in frustration at speaking the thought aloud. Her newfound, congenial tongue appeared to have its drawbacks.

***

The large hand of the store's clock ticked from eleven thirty-seven to eleven thirty-eight. Hugh paced up and down the main aisle. When he stopped by the store on his way to the bank, Charles had said to expect Violet later this morning. Well, it was later, but she hadn't arrived.

The sky hung heavy with smoky clouds that threatened to drop untold inches of snow. Without Charles to bring her in the buggy, Violet might need help transporting the rest of her goods. He looked around the empty store. The weather slowed business and afforded him an opportunity to be gone for an hour or so.

Hugh shut the ledger and slid it onto the shelf below the register. Perhaps the snow would hold off a while, and she would agree to accompany him to the café down the street for the noon meal. He longed to be with her somewhere other than his store—or tagging behind her in the middle of the night.

He untied his apron and hung it from a peg in the back room, then grabbed his hat and coat, turned the sign from *Open* to *Closed*, and locked the front door after him.

With a jaunty step and a cheerful whistle, he covered the six blocks to the street where they both lived. He slowed his pace at the sight of the carriage parked in between their houses. The horse's cocked rear leg and drooping head indicated he'd been there a sufficient time to nap. His hip flaunted the mark of the livery.

Violet entertained a guest? It would explain why she never appeared this morning.

Hugh wavered between returning to the store and traipsing up the walk to discover the identity of her visitor. Really, it was none of his business, but she did promise the rest of her delivery. He rolled his shoulders. He had a right, as a merchant colleague, to …

No. It was his duty to see that she filled the orders he had taken yesterday. It wasn't simply Violet Madison's business reputation at stake.

He marched up the porch steps and opened the screen door. Once he twisted the key on the bell, he shut the outer door, clasped his hands behind his back, and rocked on his heels until the front door opened.

"Hu … Mr. Barnes, I wasn't expecting you."

Hugh gaped at Violet. He swallowed to moisten his dry throat. He'd never seen her so … so … so soft and womanly. She wore a form-accentuating dress in a red that heightened the black in her hair. The latter was coiffed in a fashionable style complete with tiny curls surrounding her temples. She looked little like the sweet, shy Violet he'd come to know.

A blush dappled her face. "Would you like to come in? Your—"

45

Footsteps echoed on the wood flooring of the foyer as a man walked up to stand behind her. Hugh's skin turned cold and his jaw clenched with the immensity of his outrage. He shook his head at Violet. "I thought you were different."

She gasped at the growl in his voice.

What did she expect? That he would enjoy finding Kit in the company of another woman he intended to court? That he would open his arms in welcome as though a brother's betrayal was something to celebrate?

CHAPTER SIX

Seeing Kit with Violet ruined Hugh's appetite. In fact, his stomach rolled with sudden nausea. He laid the fault for his queasiness at Violet's feet. While, for him, she wore nothing but black and styled her hair in a severe manner, she'd thought nothing of changing her attire and appearance to one that would attract his brother.

He turned his anger on the man standing behind her. "What are you doing here, Kit?" Though Hugh tried to regulate his tone, he hoped his glare spoke volumes.

Something flashed in his brother's eyes also. Certainly, it couldn't be a hint of regret. "It's good to see you, too."

"Answer my question. What are you doing in Meadowmead—in Miss Madison's house?"

"He came—"

"Please stay out of this, Violet."

A frown marred Kit's good looks. "Must you be short with Miss Madison because you're angry with me?"

"After what happened between us, you have the audacity to reprimand me?"

"Only when you're wrong." If Kit's expression managed to speak aloud, it would have added, "After all, in the past you've found it necessary to point out each of my faults."

Voilet's head swiveled back and forth, trying to follow the taunts as if the men played a game of lawn tennis. This was no game, and he and Kit had said too much.

Hugh spun and descended the porch steps with heavy stomps. "Come with me, Kit. We'll discuss your arrival in private." He looked over his shoulder to make sure his brother followed.

Kit eased out the door and flashed a sheepish grin at Violet. "It was nice meeting you, Miss Madison. I appreciate the little pie."

She answered with a curt bob of her head, then pressed her palms to her cheeks. "Oh no. The tarts. What about the store, Mr. Barnes? How will I deliver my orders?"

In the past few minutes, everything he thought they'd built crashed to the ground faster than a chimney lacking mortar, and she worried about her bakery sales? "You didn't appear concerned about your orders when I found you in my brother's company, wearing a new dress and with your hair …" he waved an arm through the air, "arranged as if you were entertaining royalty."

Violet cringed and tightened her grip on the door frame. She shrank back and captured her lower lip in her teeth; then her chin dropped.

Hugh's shoulders sank, and he uncurled his fists. What had he done? Violet was not Joanna Cranston. Her head wouldn't be turned so easily. Would it?

Violet raised her chin and lifted piercing, dark eyes to meet his. The courage he'd witnessed in her lately rallied. She released the door frame and stepped forward. "This is a new dress, Mr. Barnes. I'm wearing it because I was on my way to see you when your brother arrived on my doorstep. And if you think I've acted improperly, let me assure you I invited him inside and out of the cold only because Berta was here. In return, he was kind enough to offer to transport my goods in his carriage."

Hugh's mouth opened and closed as the significance of her statement—and its frigidness—bowled him over. She had primped for him, not Kit? In a fit of jealousy, he'd humiliated her for it. With one imprudent statement, he may have destroyed her trust in him.

Lord, forgive me for my words and for treating this wonderful woman in a way that shamed both of us.

Hugh trudged up the porch steps to join her at the door. He leaned in and lowered his voice. "I'm very sorry, Violet. My remarks as well as my … my temper were uncalled for. Will you forgive me?" He hesitated. "Though I always find you lovely, you look exceptionally so today."

Her features softened and her mouth formed a silent "Oh."

He reached into the pocket of his coat, removed the

key to the store, and held it out to her. "Here. You can either wait or go without me. I'll return as soon as I can."

Their hands met as she grasped the cold metal with her equally cold fingers. Hers were soft and delicate. At their touch, he almost forgot his irritation over Kit's arrival.

"I thought you'd be pleased to see your brother. He said it's been a long time."

"Not long enough, I'm afraid."

She clutched the key in a fist. "Is there anything I can do?"

"There is one thing." Hugh glanced over his shoulder, then turned back to Violet. "Keep away from Kit."

***

Keep away from his brother? Why?

With one look at Christopher … Kit … Barnes, Hugh, a man of gentle temperament, had turned into someone with a savage countenance, curled fists, and a cold voice capable of freezing Widener's Pond in August. Violet had never known him to be rude or lose his temper. In that short space of time, she hadn't recognized the man, nor had she liked him much.

Nevertheless, it took only an apology to restore her faith in his virtues. After all, she lost her temper that morning, so who was she to throw stones?

"Please, Violet. I'll explain later."

Her thoughts veered to the man at the end of the path. Yes, he was handsome and charming, but he was not the one who held an attraction for her that could never be dulled by another. "All right."

He covered the hand containing the key and rubbed his thumb across her skin, creating a flutter in her middle that left her feeling as though she might fly. The contact lasted but a moment before he stomped down the front path to his brother. Both men marched toward Hugh's house.

Violet had scarcely caught her breath when another carriage stopped out front. Her future sister-in-law climbed down and hurried along the front path. Once she reached the porch, Lila said, "Is something wrong? Who is the gentleman with Mr. Barnes?"

"Nothing is wrong. The man is his brother." Violet opened the screen door for a third time that morning and gestured her inside. "I wasn't expecting you."

Lila inspected her hair and then the dress. "What a lovely shade on you. I've never seen you wear it. And your hair … You might not have awaited my arrival, but it's obvious you expected a visitor. Or perhaps two?"

"No, I …" She snapped her mouth shut on Lila's teasing. The past few minutes had strained her emotions sufficiently. The last thing she wanted was to defend herself to Lila. "I'm sorry, but I'm on my way to deliver my orders to the grocery store and don't have much time."

Lila sauntered into the parlor and looked around. "I know. Charles is worried about you. He said you weren't quite yourself this morning and asked me to drive you to the grocer's because it looks like snow."

Dear, interfering Charles.

"I must admit, seeing Mr. Barnes and his brother put a fright in me. I was afraid Charles had reason to worry."

A closer connection with Lila over the past week had begun to crumble the wall of reserve Violet had built around her feelings for her future sister-in-law. The genuine concern in Lila's words and voice sped the process. "I'm fine. There's no need for either of you to be troubled on my account. But I am in a hurry, so ..."

Lila waved a hand through the air. "Well then, let's get you and your cakes to the grocer's." She disappeared into the kitchen before Violet could thank her for understanding or correct her assumption about the type of desserts she'd made.

Lila parked the carriage along the street in front of Hugh's store. Snow drifted down in large, slow flakes. She peered at the door. "Mr. Barnes is still gone. The *Closed* sign is up."

"He gave me the key."

"He did, did he?" Lila turned on the seat, a glint of speculation in her eyes. "Mr. Barnes must think highly of you to trust you with a key to his store."

Violet escaped the carriage and her soon-to-be sister-in-law's uncomfortable inspection. Hugh said he'd explain his cryptic warning. But did he think highly enough of her to reveal the full story behind both his animosity toward Kit and his obvious jealousy?

In her whole adult life, she had not imagined a man experiencing jealousy over her. She pinched her wrist. The pain assured her she wasn't dreaming.

After toting the basket of tarts to the building, she poked the key into the lock. Though she had slipped back into a timid state over Hugh's anger, in the end she stood up for herself. How happy she was to not be the same Shrinking Violet of even a week ago. But would her newfound courage get her everything she wanted … including Hugh Barnes?

***

Hugh owed Violet more than an apology. If he desired a deeper relationship with her than friendship, he owed her the truth, something he dreaded revealing.

He removed his coat and hung it from a hook in the hall tree, using the time to gain a stronger hold on his simmering anger.

His brother removed his hat and stepped past Hugh to stand in the center of the foyer. He twisted one way to view the parlor, then the other to inspect the smaller sitting room Hugh used as an office. "Nice house."

Hugh hung his hat on a second hook and walked into the parlor to stand by the front window, too tense to sit. "Now that I know you approve of where I live, what is it you want?"

Kit settled into the nearest chair, crossed his legs, and propped his hat on his knee. After a moment of silence, he said, "Forgiveness."

"We discussed this situation five years ago. You're forgiven." Even as he spoke, Hugh recognized the statement as a lie. Forgiving his brother meant a renewal of their relationship. Now that he'd met Violet, he dreaded risking a repeat of the past. Why should he open himself to more turmoil involving Kit?

"Yes, I could see that by the way you treated Miss Madison." Kit's knee bounced in quick succession in the short silence that followed his sarcasm. "What I did was wrong, Hugh. I knew it at the time. I wish I could say my seduction of Joanna resulted from a love for her, but it didn't. It was pure reprisal for your judgment and interference in my activities. I decided to mete out what I considered an appropriate punishment. In the end, I ruined a future for both you and the lady you'd chosen.

"I'm not the same man I was five years ago, big brother. Christ not only saved my soul, He saved me from drink and the other many sins I've committed throughout my lifetime. He forgave me once and for all. How many times must I beg your forgiveness?"

The breath whooshed from Hugh's lungs. His wayward brother had found salvation? He no longer drank?

While Kit rested a steady hand on the arm of the chair, Hugh studied him for any sign of deceit. Clean-shaven and well-dressed, Kit watched him in turn through eyes that were clear and alert. Hugh crossed the room, stopped before his brother, and sniffed, not bothering to disguise the action. Soap. Hair tonic. None of the typical liquor fumes.

Kit huffed. "Satisfied?"

"You've professed rehabilitation on various occasions in the past, usually when you're in some kind of trouble. How can I be sure you're telling the truth this time?"

"The only way I know to prove it to you is through time and observation. So if you'll allow me the time, I have no objections to being observed." Kit chuckled. "Don't get me wrong, I'm not perfect. On the other hand, it's been twenty-seven months since I've sipped a drop of liquor. I don't trifle with the affections of the ladies, and I'm no longer the moral image of our father. It's taken me a long time to get up the nerve to come see you face-to-face and reiterate how truly sorry I am for my part in your unhappiness."

Notwithstanding the physical evidence, a little voice insisted his brother claimed to have changed too much for it to be real. The break with Kit and Joanna, the woman Hugh once thought he would marry, prompted a move from Philadelphia five years ago. It eventually led him to Meadowmead, where he'd met Violet. During those years, God had worked in a majestic way in his life. Why shouldn't his brother receive healing from the demon of alcohol and the temptation of the flesh?

Still …

Kit rose from his seat and faced Hugh. "There is something else you should know."

Ah, now it comes out. Hugh braced himself.

"God will use our history, our experiences, to accomplish His will. In Pittsburgh, I've started a home for those who seek the same peace and sobriety I've found. I also minister to men with families, trying to assist the ones who can't seem to give up the alcohol while organizing aid for wives and children.

"If you allow me to stay for a few weeks, you'll see that I've changed. I'll use the time I'm here to continue my ministry, and I won't go inside any drinking establishments." He lowered his head. "It's too difficult for me. That doesn't mean you won't hear of me in the vicinity of a tavern, or see me near one yourself."

Even while a tiny corner of his spirit begged him to give his brother the benefit of the doubt, Hugh's distrust refused to vanish completely. "As you said, I'll observe."

Kit held out a hand. "That's all I can ask of you."

Hugh stared at the outstretched hand. After several seconds, he clasped it, praying he wasn't risking his future with Violet by trusting in his brother's reformation.

CHAPTER SEVEN

"Thank you, Mrs. Green." Within minutes of Violet's opening the door to Hugh's grocery, the woman arrived to pick up the specially ordered apple cake. Violet recorded the purchase in her ledger and added the payment to the cash register drawer.

"I'm sure you're finding yourself quite busy with Christmas festivities this time of year." The woman's rounded cheeks rose.

"Yes, ma'am." Thanks to teas and evening fetes—and Mrs. Julian's effusive advertising—sales had been brisk. The true test would come after the holidays when Violet would discover whether or not her recipes garnered the money she required to live on her own.

"You should open your own bakery, Miss Madison. This town has lacked one for too long."

Dare she agree out loud? Like her ministry to the poor, Violet believed God had guided her in beginning this enterprise, so why be hesitant? She took a deep breath. "I am considering it."

"Good. Times are changing, and the opportunities for women to show they have a head for business are growing. Look how well we run our own homes." She clucked her tongue. "If only those in power would allow us the vote."

Violet's father always said proper voting demanded logic over emotion, and women were too emotional. Did she even want the responsibility of choosing the right candidates to represent her in vital government positions?

Mrs. Green turned to leave, then snapped her fingers. "While I'm here, I'll pick up a few things I forgot last time."

Violet caught her breath. Pick up a few things? She hadn't come to operate Hugh's store in his absence. What would he say if he discovered she had presumed to take over his business? "Mrs. Green …"

"Yes?"

"I …" Why should Hugh lose sales during the time she waited here? If she wanted to run a bakery—or vote at some point in the future—it was high time she learned to take charge of unexpected situations. "Please, go ahead."

Lila snickered from a few feet away.

Violet dragged Hugh's heavy ledger from a shelf under the register, found the price list he kept inside, and hoped it was current. She also found four more orders. At this rate, she'd need another oven to keep up.

Charles already complained that Berta must fit her meal preparations in between "… the rising and the frosting of Violet's confounded cakes." Once he married, his family's requirements would come first—

as they should—which meant she must find another location for both her home and her baking.

One thought led to another until she began daydreaming about living in the house next door to the one in which she'd grown up, and baking for the man who—

"What are you doing?"

Violet flinched. "What?"

Lila joined her behind the counter and pointed at Violet's hands. She had been rubbing a thumb over the top of her other hand, as Hugh had done earlier and, based on Lila's amused reaction, she had probably been doing so with a rapturous look on her face.

Mrs. Green returned with a half dozen purchases, saving Violet the embarrassment of searching for a suitable answer to Lila's question.

Violet recorded everything in the book, took Mrs. Green's money, and wished her a happy Christmas.

"It's been a pleasure to speak with you, Miss Madison. Mind you, I expect to patronize your bakery soon."

A rush of satisfaction filled Violet as the woman toddled out the door.

"I have to agree." Lila stepped up to the counter. "Charles doesn't like the idea of you starting a business, but I think it's refreshing to see you no longer hiding in that house."

The coins clinked as Violet dropped them into the appropriate sections of the register drawer. "Hiding?

What do you mean?"

"It's no secret that your father kept you under glass, treating you like a flower too delicate for life in the world."

Too delicate for the world? "It's true that I've never been one to socialize, but you make it sound as if he kept me prisoner." Violet slammed the cash register drawer shut, irritated that too much truth rested in the assumption.

Lila tilted her head. "I'm sure he loved you and meant well."

"Yes, he did love me. He told me often that he waited for the right man, one who would overlook my plain appearance and timidity." Poor Father hadn't expected his heart to give out first. And why was she sharing such personal information?

Lila clamped her lips, then swirled her gloved palm with a flourish. "Look at you now. A few days ago you wore only black and would have found it difficult to say hello to Mrs. Green. Today you conducted business with her in a confident manner. You're like a whole new woman. I'm proud of you, Violet Madison."

Proud or urging her out of the nest? A quick study of Lila's smile convinced Violet that she meant what she said. It also raised a disturbing question. Had she allowed fear to distort her future sister-in-law's words and actions these past months?

Violet glanced out the plate-glass window at the wet, white blanket covering the back of Lila's horse. "It's snowing harder. I wouldn't want your buggy to slide off the road on your way home."

Lila followed her gaze. "Lock up and come with me. I doubt anyone else will shop in this weather."

"I'll wait a little longer." After all she'd gone through this morning, if her customer didn't come for the tarts, Violet would deliver them to the woman's house, even if she had to wear snowshoes. Besides, she wanted to be here when Hugh returned.

"Fine, but at least tell Charles I tried." Lila opened the door and stopped. Flakes of snow blew inside and melted into a puddle along the threshold. "You'll have time to make my wedding cake, won't you, Violet?"

She longed to ease the concern in the woman's voice. "No order is more important."

"Good." Lila shook a finger at her. "Mark my words, Mr. Barnes fits the description of the man your father waited for. Before long you'll have him so infatuated he'll sweep you off to that dreamland you were in a few minutes ago."

Violet's stomach dropped. Were her feelings so transparent? And what if Lila was wrong?

***

Hugh lumbered back to the store with snow falling all around him. At least two inches had accumulated in the time he'd left Violet standing open-mouthed at her door until now. Hoof prints and dark lines from passing carriages rutted the white streets, but traffic was sparse.

 61

He rounded the corner onto Main Street and, for the last block, ducked his head to shield his face from a renewal of the heavy flakes.

After opening the door and stomping the snow from his shoes, Hugh entered the grocery and stood mesmerized by the sweet laughter coming from across the room—Violet's laughter, as light and clear as a spoon tapped against fine crystal.

"You tell a funny story, Mr. Sweeney." Outfitted in the red dress with its black trim, Violet perched like a cardinal on the eight-foot ladder along the wall. She reached sideways for a box on a shelf.

Once his brain confirmed the unnerving sight, Hugh rushed to hold the ladder. At his abrupt grasp, it wobbled, and the laughter changed to a high-pitched screech.

"Careful, Miss Madison."

She peered down at him. "I was fine until a moment ago, Mr. Barnes."

"My fault, Barnes. I asked the nice lady to hand me some of them raisins up there." Meadowmead's barber slapped the leg injured in the war over twenty-five years earlier. He'd limped ever since. "I ain't up to climbing, and the wife wants to stock the larder with supplies for Christmas dinner."

"Don't worry, Mr. Sweeney. It's my fault. I should have replaced this rickety ladder long ago. Seeing Miss Madison climb it almost caused me apoplexy." He'd go to the hardware store down the street first thing tomorrow morning.

Violet descended the rungs, box in hand, and passed the raisins off to the man. "Is that all, Mr. Sweeney?"

"That'll do it, missy."

She led him to the counter and began to record the sale as if she were an employee of the store … or the owner. Hugh waited with his arms crossed while amusement danced through him.

Violet looked up and caught him watching. She glanced down at the ledger, then back at him. "Oh." She dropped the pen and shuffled two steps to the left. "You should do this."

Hugh joined her behind the counter and peered at the recordings in the book. In the past two hours, she had filled nearly half a page with purchased items. The sales weren't as strong as on a normal day, but with the weather to slow things down, it was more than he'd expected. He checked the prices she'd charged, nodded his approval, and backed away. "Please, continue."

Flashing a quick smile at Mr. Sweeney, Violet picked up the pen and resumed the work she'd started. Finally, the barber left and Hugh turned the card hanging from a nail at the top of the door, then locked up the store for the day.

He walked back to Violet. "I stopped by your house to retrieve the key. Berta said you weren't there." He pointed to the ledger. "Now, I know why."

She ducked her chin. "I only meant to help."

He reached out and tipped her head up, pleased

when she didn't evade his touch. "And I'm grateful for it. You've done a fine job this afternoon."

She rewarded him with a broad smile that turned his insides to steaming mush. The effect urged him to draw closer to her. *Look away.* He yearned to feel the warmth of her lips on his. Would he frighten her if he acted upon the impulse?

He withdrew his hand and stepped back. "I'll walk you home in a few minutes, but how about a cup of coffee or tea to warm you first?"

"That would be nice."

A few minutes later, he set a cup on the counter in front of Violet and pulled up a stool for her. While he'd prepared fresh coffee, she cut them each a slice of chocolate cake. His mouth watered at the sight. "You really should have gone home before the snow fell in earnest, but I'm glad you're here."

They ate and drank and spoke of agreeable subjects as if the troubling event of the morning had never happened. As much as he wished it, he couldn't avoid the subject for all time.

Once he'd finished both the cake and coffee, he pushed the cup and plate away. She waited in silence while he organized his thoughts and searched for the proper words. Finally, he released a heavy breath. "Violet, the way I treated you this morning was inexcusable, but if you'd let me, I'd like to explain what prompted my anger."

"Please do."

Would she even want to be his friend after she discovered his background?

"My parents met in Philadelphia thirty years ago. Mother grew up in a wealthy household. Father was the son of a butcher. She was taken in by his good looks."

"Taken in?"

"My father has never been a scrupulous person, but she didn't bother to look deeper than the outer shell. As you can imagine, my maternal grandfather opposed their marriage, their social differences being only one of the many reasons. Father drank to excess even before the wedding, and it got worse afterward. Not long into the marriage, he ... he began to indulge in the admiration of other women." What a polite way to put the adultery that went on under his mother's nose.

Rather than turning away in shock or disgust, Violet sat quietly, her hands folded in her lap, her concentration trained on him. "The marriage lasted only long enough to leave my mother with two boys to raise."

"How sad." She pulled a handkerchief from her skirt pocket and balled it in her fist.

On other occasions, Hugh had noted her habit of twisting and tugging it in times of tension. She had a gentle and sympathetic heart, and he fully expected her to make proper use of the lace-edged cloth by the end of his tale.

He rubbed his forehead. "Sometimes, I believe we all would have been better off if they'd never met."

"In that case, you and I would have missed the opportunity to be friends."

 65

Leave it to The Angel to cheer him by seeing the good in a detestable situation. He clasped her hand. "For my part, I'd consider that a tragedy."

"As would I."

How deep did her friendship go? Deeper than he dared hope?

Her soothing, brown eyes held his captive until he remembered they sat in full view of anyone passing by the store's large windows. He released her hand and cleared his throat. "Afterward, we lived with my grandparents. Grandfather Mullins wasn't an easy man to please. He and Kit tended to square up to one another on a regular basis. My brother took after our father both in looks and character, but Mother doted on him."

Hugh paused to judge the wisdom of revealing all. Violet's light touch on his arm encouraged him to divulge the rest. "I'm as much to blame as my grandfather for Kit following in our father's footsteps."

"Why would you say that?"

"Since his teen years, he'd come home intoxicated. He followed the wrong crowd and got into trouble. I'd help him cover his actions while chastising him for them." Hugh rolled his tense shoulders. "Kit resented my interference, but I was too self-righteous to realize that each time I scolded him he did something worse."

"That finally drove you two apart?"

"It was the root cause. The last time I saw my brother was five years ago. I caught him and …" When her fingers pulled at the handkerchief, shame and trepidation prevented him from looking her in the face. "He was with the woman I'd planned to marry."

With a slow turn of his head, he grimaced at Violet's hands as she twisted the handkerchief into tight knots.

CHAPTER EIGHT

The gray and white landscape glittered in the moonlight as Violet tramped through the snow toward the front gate of her home. The bottom edges of her dress and quilted petticoat were soaked already. By the time she finished her rounds, the hems would be frozen and tug on her waist as if she'd lined them with fishing weights.

Three hours earlier, she had gone to bed with the thought of staying home on this cold Wednesday night. After tossing and turning with the internal call to carry out her mission, she changed her mind.

She was The Yuletide Angel and people needed her.

Hauling three more flour sacks of food, she meant to carry out tonight's deliveries with haste before the toes covered by two pairs of wool stockings and a pair of boots turned numb.

And before leftover fear discouraged her.

More than likely, an animal had made the noise she'd heard last week. Tonight, she carried her father's hickory walking stick for protection from whatever, or whomever, might lurk in the shadows.

Violet stopped in front of Hugh's darkened house.

The sight of it rekindled the memory of his revelation about his family. It didn't excuse his reaction when seeing her with Kit, but now she understood the cause. That understanding created a dull ache inside.

Even though Kit had apologized, claiming to have found salvation, Hugh doubted his brother's sincerity and harbored an unforgiving attitude in his heart. What would she do in similar circumstances?

Father, for Hugh's sake, I pray for his willingness to grant his brother forgiveness. In the name of Jesus, I ask for reconciliation between them and restoration of their brotherly bond.

Recalling Hugh had once considered marriage to someone else sparked the sting of hurt and jealousy. She found comfort in a reminder that she'd heard no lingering affection for the woman in Hugh's voice. In fact, more than once yesterday she had sensed his desire to …

Despite the cold air blowing against her cheeks and nose, Violet's face grew warm. Had he wanted to kiss her yesterday, or was she simply reacting to her own eagerness to be kissed by him?

She lifted her face and squinted at the tiny glow of light coming from a second-floor window in Hugh's house. It lasted little more than a second before it died out, but in that time, the corner of a curtain appeared to drop.

Violet dismissed the uncomfortable notion of being watched from that window. Both men were asleep. No one had seen her.

For the next hour, Violet's senses tingled with unease and her gaze darted here and there, searching the shadows. She glanced over her shoulder or stopped to listen for the crunch of snow from someone else's footsteps. Dogs barked. A baby cried.

Twice an ill-defined shape moved in the distance, and she froze, waiting and watching. She gripped the walking stick until her fingers ached.

Silence. She hurried on.

Once she had dropped her gifts at each house, she rushed home, changed clothes, and climbed underneath the chilled bedcovers. In a matter of minutes, she'd forgotten her earlier anxiety and fell asleep to the satisfaction that grew with each visit by The Yuletide Angel.

***

Garlands of holly, strands of strung cranberries, and red ribbon served as the floral ornamentation for the wedding of Violet's brother and Lila Blackstone. The colorful additions decorated the fireplace mantles and doorways of the rooms in the Madison house and would remain until after Christmas.

How odd that Violet had dreaded this day until it arrived. Now that the vows had been exchanged, a surprising peace settled over her.

She set the plate with the double tiers of white wedding cake on the dining room table. Rather than send guests home with a slice in small boxes, Lila had chosen to feed them here, and Violet offered to serve them.

During the past week, she had spent hours practicing the edible decorations on paper until assured of her ability to pipe icing borders and form leaves and flowers to Lila's exact specifications.

"Ah, Lila said I'd be impressed by the cake." Hugh sidled up beside her and studied the confection.

"This is the first time I've ever undertaken such an elaborate project. Personally, I would settle for a simpler design. Perhaps shell piping and a bouquet of tiny rose buds at one end of the top layer." Violet closed her eyes and saw it in her mind.

She held a silver knife, ready to slice through the bottom layer. The vision took an unexpected turn when Hugh pressed behind her, reached around, and enclosed her hand in his. Her eyes popped open. Her skin tingled where he'd caressed the top of her hand—in her dream.

She shook her head, mortified by the image and her unsolicited candor about the cake. "I-I didn't mean to sound critical of Lila's choice."

"You didn't. You sounded like a woman who's given a great deal of thought to a momentous occasion. Are you hoping to marry one day, Violet?"

Her breath hitched, but his earnestness prompted her to answer with honesty. "Yes. I have dreams of a home and family of my own."

"What about your intention to open a bakery?"

Would Hugh approve of his wife owning a business? "I'd like to think the man who loves me will choose to become a partner in my endeavors."

He glanced around, then bent closer. "As the first mate on your sailing ship?"

Violet drew back. He remembered her comment from days ago about sailing a schooner? "No. As a co-captain."

Hugh stood silent. Perhaps she should have been more prudent, but something in the way he watched her—as if he longed for her opinion—had spurred her on.

"I'm certain the man who loves you will gladly choose to stand alongside you at the helm."

She had little experience with flirtation and even less with true romantic statements, but the turn in their conversation weakened her knees.

"Well, it appears you have confirmed my daughter's faith in your talent." Her brother's new mother-in-law, a willowy woman whose oval face was an older version of Lila's, joined them at the table and broke the charm of the moment.

"Thank you, Mrs. Blackstone."

She wrapped an arm around Violet's waist. "Now that we're family, I hope to see more of you, dear. In fact, you must come with Charles and Lila for supper at our home on Christmas Eve. It will be a small gathering, about a dozen."

As a tradition, the Madisons attended a church

service on Christmas Eve, then returned home to a quiet supper Violet had prepared in advance for her father, her brother, and herself. Why hadn't it occurred to her that Lila and Charles would make other plans this year, forge a new tradition?

With her father gone and the vows barely spoken, the charity began.

As soon as the unkind opinion materialized, she rejected it. Her life no longer revolved around her brother's generosity and duty. God had provided her with new opportunities, and she planned to make the most of them.

"I'd be happy to bring a dessert."

"Lovely." Mrs. Blackstone turned to Hugh. "We would be delighted if you and your brother celebrated the holy birth with us, Mr. Barnes."

"I'd be honored, ma'am." After a quick glance at Violet, his bearing stiffened. "And I'll extend the invitation to Kit."

A few minutes later, Berta dipped punch into the cups while Violet served the cake to almost two dozen guests who mingled about the first floor of the Madison home. The volume of people's voices rose and fell around her, but she paid little notice to the conversations. She contemplated her work … and Hugh. Rather than move about the rooms to socialize, he stayed nearby, as if he waited for an occasion to continue their earlier discussion.

Really, her feet might as well be six inches off the

ground. How could this enchantment with him have developed so quickly, and where would it lead? He had not asked permission to court her and, based on his previous insistence to remain a bachelor, he might never do so. She suspected his past experience with love to be the source of his commitment to an unmarried state. But why had he been so interested in her marital dreams?

Two gentlemen, employees of the bank where Charles worked, stopped on the other side of the table. One said, "I suppose the snow kept our local Samaritan away on Wednesday night."

Violet halted the knife as it slid halfway through the next slice of cake. *He thinks snow kept The Angel away?*

The other man laughed. "It probably weighed down his wings and the poor fellow couldn't fly from house to house."

"More likely, he's not as goodhearted as everyone insists if he let a little snow keep him from his rounds. What a shame."

Not goodhearted? Violet pressed her lips together to keep from informing them of the difficulty she'd faced trudging through five inches of snow. Despite being wrapped in her warmest clothes and with a scarf around her face, the cold had numbed her ears, toes, and fingers by the time she returned home.

She slapped cake slices on plates and handed them to the men. With the barest of appreciation, they received the cake and moved on.

"I wonder if they've ever made an effort to see to the needs of others." Hugh glared at the men's backs as they ambled off, guffawing over their joke.

While his defense warmed Violet's heart, her thoughts shifted to the substance of the men's remarks. By now, people should be buzzing with the news of another visit by The Yuletide Angel. Instead, the talk she'd heard in the past few days centered on the fact that no one reported receiving their gifts. How could that be when she had left them in plain sight?

Were people growing too accustomed to her deliveries? She gritted her teeth. Did they take them for granted and no longer see the effort as special?

***

After the wedding and reception, Hugh returned to the store. He'd risked revealing his feelings to Violet, and in public no less, but he'd grown weary of not knowing for sure where she stood on marriage. Violet's forthright answers strengthened his decision to ask to court her after the Christmas celebrations.

He chuckled. "Co-captains sailing through life together. What an adventure."

"Did you say something, Mr. Barnes?"

He glanced up. His customer's pinched lips hinted at restrained merriment. "Uh ... pardon me, ma'am. I was talking to myself."

Once the woman left, he closed the store and started in the opposite direction of his house, taking a lazy, roundabout walk in the brisk air. He approached the jeweler's shop, and his steps slowed to a near halt. What would Violet say if he presented her with an engagement ring as a Christmas gift?

He glanced around to be sure he was alone, stepped closer, then backed away and continued his stroll. The last thing he needed was someone questioning why he chose to look in this particular window.

His nose grew cold, but the temperature this afternoon wasn't as frigid as in the early hours of the morning when he'd traipsed through the darkness to follow Violet. One more night, Christmas Eve, and The Yuletide Angel would disappear for another year.

At the thought, his steps faltered, and he nearly tripped over his feet. The Angel would disappear in another week, but it appeared her latest gifts had already done so. Why hadn't people admitted to having received the sacks Violet left the other night? He had seen her place the bags at three homes. So why were no deliveries reported? Strange.

Even stranger, it appeared she'd suspected someone followed her, because she stopped twice to listen, but never turned in his direction. The past two Wednesdays were unlike the first when she journeyed with confidence between houses … without carrying the walking stick. He must be more careful next week, or she might use it on him.

Minutes later, he turned the corner and jerked to a stop. Kit stood outside the tavern alongside Wendell

Collinsworth. The men laughed together, looking like two old friends.

Hugh's nostrils flared, and his lips curled. He had tried to give Kit the benefit of the doubt. He'd prayed his brother had changed, but Kit lied to him. He hadn't changed one bit. He still enjoyed the company of drunkards and, possibly, a thief.

For the past several weeks, Hugh had kept a close watch on Collinsworth. Though he had no proof, he suspected the man was responsible for the merchandise disappearing from his store. Twice he'd become aware of something missing on the same day the man visited.

His feet pounded the ground as he marched forward. The men's laughter died at his approach.

"Do you have something to tell me, Kit?"

His brother frowned. "I'm talking to Wendell."

Hugh glanced between the two men while a flicker of doubt sparked. His temper snuffed it out. "I noticed."

"I guess I'll mosey on." Wendell turned and stumbled inside the tavern.

Kit's forehead puckered. "Why did you interrupt?"

"You told me you'd stopped drinking," Hugh jabbed his finger toward the building, "and look where I found you."

"Did you see me come out of there?"

The spark of misgiving flamed a second time. "No, but—"

"But you assumed. What I said was the truth. If you'll remember, I also mentioned I would continue my ministry while I was here, and you might see me in this type of situation." Kit ran a hand over his face in a sign of frustration. "I almost had Wendell convinced he should return to his niece and nephew. They're worried about him. Now, I'll be forced to tell Mitch it will be hours before his uncle arrives home."

At Kit's tight expression, Hugh wanted to slink down the street. So far, he'd let his past hurt overrule any burgeoning faith in his brother's changed life. If they were going to repair their relationship, he must afford Kit a chance to prove himself. He must forgive no matter how hard. "I'm sorry. I'm learning that trust is not easily restored once lost. I suppose it will be impossible if I never make the effort."

Kit relaxed his stance and released a drawn-out sigh. "I can't blame you, Hugh. I brought it on myself. I'll tell you once more that those days are gone and ask you to believe in me."

Hugh hesitated. The old doubts grew and tried to choke out his desire to forgive his brother. He shoved them aside. "I'll talk to Wendell."

He started up the tavern steps, but Kit grabbed his arm. "Forget it. If you're inclined to help, you can go with me to talk to the children."

"All right. Let's stop at the store and gather a few things first."

They reached the Collinsworth shack, not surprised to find Wendell remained gone. Hugh set a box of food on the table. He scowled as he emptied the box and placed the items on a shelf alongside a number of other canned goods. It didn't mean Wendell hadn't bought the food, but Hugh doubted it.

When he finished, he stood at one end of a large space that served as kitchen and sitting room. Kit crouched and took the hand of each child. "All we can do is pray for your uncle."

The little girl bobbed her head, but Mitch grew stiff-necked. "I heard Mama say he'd never amount to nothin'. Guess she was right."

"People can change, Mitch, but they have to want it more than their sin. I believe your uncle will eventually come to that realization." Kit clamped a hand on Mitch's shoulder. "In the meantime, I'll be in town for a while. If you need anything, find me, day or night."

Both children wrapped their arms around Kit. For the first time, Hugh fully comprehended the compassion that drove Violet to assume the identity of The Yuletide Angel and his brother to minister to those whose present circumstances reflected his past.

As more comforting words poured from Kit, the unforgiving glacier in Hugh's heart began to melt. A new brother crouched on the floor, a new creation.

CHAPTER NINE

The time crept to eleven while Lila played carols on the piano. Many of the Blackstones' Christmas Eve guests patted their knees to the music. Some hummed or sang along. It was Violet who entertained Hugh.

For the sixth time in the past half hour, she glanced at the clock on the parlor mantle and frowned. Her right knee bounced under the layers of skirts. He raised a hand and covered his amusement. Either she possessed no sense of rhythm or she tapped her toe in impatience. How many sacks did she plan to deliver tonight? Another three?

An uncomfortable foreboding had gripped Hugh off and on all evening. Most of the time, he'd successfully wrested it away. Thank goodness, after tonight, he need not worry over Violet. But what about next year? Hopefully, they would distribute the gifts together—as man and wife.

A large tree occupied the space next to the piano. Candles glowed on the branches and illuminated various ornaments in the shapes of balls and stars. Lila led them in singing a rollicking version of *Jolly Old Saint Nicholas*. An appropriate choice to follow his thoughts on this Christmas Eve.

Once the music ended, Violet jumped from her seat. She turned to her host and hostess. "It's been a lovely evening, Mr. and Mrs. Blackstone. Thank you for inviting me."

Mrs. Blackstone gripped Violet's hand. "It was our pleasure, but must you leave so early?"

"I'm afraid so." Her laughter rang high and false. "Santa Claus is on his way."

This time Hugh released the pent up humor only to have Violet glower at him.

Her brother gathered the ladies' coats. Violet grabbed hers and said, "Please don't leave on my account, Charles."

"Someone must see you home. It's not far, but a lady doesn't roam the streets alone at night."

Before he embarrassed himself with more exploding laughter at Charles' innocent comment, Hugh stepped forward. "Kit and I should leave, too. With your permission, we'll be happy to escort your sister home."

Violet paused in the act of fastening the clasps on her coat. Her glance caught Hugh's, and its softness conveyed silent approval—perhaps mixed with urgency? It was a forthright look he couldn't imagine her giving anyone a month ago. Or had he read too much into their unspoken exchange?

Charles hesitated, shifting his attention from Hugh to Violet to Kit and back to Hugh. In the interim, Lila stepped forward. "I think that's a fine idea. Charles and

I had planned to give my parents their Christmas gift this evening, so we'd like to stay a while longer."

"All the more reason we should leave." Violet wished everyone a "Merry Christmas," and Hugh followed her out the door.

Before descending the porch steps, he offered her his arm. "Take care that you don't slip."

With Violet settled beside him on the front seat of the carriage, he left the back seat for his brother. Once they reached the curb in front of her house, the carriage wobbled as Kit jumped out. Hugh tensed when his brother reached for Violet's hand to help her to the ground, but he brushed aside the twinge of mistrust.

"You're safe now, Miss Violet." Kit pressed the fingers covered by her glove and winked at Hugh. "Since it doesn't take two of us to see you to your door, I'll leave the task to my brother while I take care of the horse." He climbed back in the carriage and reined the animal toward the small barn at the rear of the property.

As he did when leaving the Blackstones', Hugh slipped Violet's arm through his and strolled up the walk. She might be in a hurry to make her final rounds, but he was in no hurry to let her leave his side. "An enjoyable evening, don't you think?"

"Lovely."

The hollow space under the porch boards resounded with their footsteps in the quiet darkness. The apprehension of trouble-to-come latched on to Hugh once more and refused to let go. "Violet ..." How could he warn her away from her planned activity without revealing his knowledge of it?

"Yes?"

At the eagerness in her expression, he replaced the worry with the first words that came to mind. "Merry Christmas, my beautiful Violet."

***

My beautiful Violet.

She floated inside the house and up the stairs, reliving Hugh's goodnight over and over until she entered her bedroom. She stood in the middle of the room and pressed her fingers to her mouth. Hugh Barnes called her beautiful.

Happy tears spilled as she removed the evening dress, hung it in the wardrobe, and donned the old black frock she wore as The Yuletide Angel. She wiped the moisture away with the back of her hand as his parting words rolled through her mind. *"Take care and stay safe."* The admonition drew her up short. Safe from what?

The words were not as alarming as the tone in which they were delivered and the concern on his handsome face. Did he think she was in danger from something? Or did he know of her plan for this night? She had wanted to ask, but the words wouldn't pass her lips for fear she was wrong and would raise suspicions in him that weren't there beforehand. More than likely, he simply issued a farewell, similar to wishing her sweet dreams.

She frowned. Only he didn't say sweet dreams. He told her to stay safe.

Violet dropped to her hands and knees and reached under the bed for the final three sacks she would deliver. She didn't understand why no one mentioned receiving her gifts last week. Was charity no longer news? Well, thanklessness would not keep her from her calling.

After grabbing her father's walking stick, she left the house before Charles and Lila returned.

***

Violet stuck to the shadows and out of sight of anyone in the homes she passed. She reached for the door of the first house on her list. It belonged to a war veteran who'd fallen on hard times. A proud man, he refused ordinary charity. But who could refuse what The Yuletide Angel left?

Something rustled in the nearby bushes. She glanced around as the eeriness of being watched returned. Whatever was out there, the darkness hid it.

Maybe it was St. Nick. A nervous snicker escaped her throat. *Silly goose.*

She set the sack inside and moved on, passing through the town's small park to her next destination. The perception of menace grew stronger as she lowered the second gift. Her skin crawled with the sense that someone lurked nearby.

More rustling.

Take care and stay safe.

 84

Violet dropped both sacks and whirled. She whipped up her skirts in one hand and brandished the walking stick in the other. She took two steps and crashed headlong into a dark figure standing in the pathway. Arms reached for her. She raised the weapon in her hand and struck out. The stick cracked against flesh and bone.

Her attacker hollered and a mixture of familiar odors filled the air between them. The strident voice raised an alarm in her head. Violet had no time to even glance up. The villain knocked her backward and she lost her balance. She twisted and tried to catch herself as she hit the ground.

Pain shot up her left arm and her scream tore through the night air.

***

Kit wanted to talk—about their mother, the past, the future—all while Hugh imagined Violet preparing for her next jaunt along the darkened streets of Meadowmead. His pulse raced with the urgency to leave without raising suspicion in Kit. As a result, he missed the opportunity to follow right away after spotting her leaving the Madison house.

Finally, he feigned a yawn. "Well, I guess it's time we went upstairs."

Kit glanced at the clock on the mantle, slapped his knees, and rose from the parlor chair in which he'd sprawled. "I didn't realize it was so late."

 85

The two of them plodded up the stairs and drifted into their own rooms. Once he heard Kit's bedroom door click shut, Hugh crept out of his room still wearing his evening attire. Come Monday, he expected his laundry woman to scold him over the mud-splattered trousers. He slipped down the stairs, grabbed his coat and hat from the hall tree, and went out the door without looking back.

In the past, Violet had traveled in a circular pattern around the town. Why no one else recognized that orderly habit of The Angel's continued to confound him. He guessed at the neighborhood she might prowl tonight and jogged east, even now fighting the portent of a disaster in the making.

He took a shortcut through the park. When he reached the corner of Jacob and Harris Streets, he stopped to catch his breath while deciding which direction best allowed him to cross her path.

A yell broke the silence around him. A second later, a scream rent the night. If possible, every hair underneath Hugh's bowler stood at attention.

He bolted through the blackness to save his beloved Violet.

CHAPTER TEN

Regardless of the pain shooting through her arm, Violet wiggled into a sitting position on the ground. She pressed her left arm to her abdomen and with her right, raised the walking stick and swung it.

It sliced the air with a *whoosh*, narrowly missing the man's head. She slashed at her attacker repeatedly. He sidestepped, and she missed. As she swung her arm backward, prepared to try once more, he grabbed the two sacks and dashed into the nearby trees.

Violet struggled through the pain to rise to her feet as sleepy-eyed adults wearing robes and coats over their night shirts and gowns encircled her. Men held lanterns that produced golden rings of light to illuminate the area, while two children stared up at her.

"What's all the commotion?" A bearded man stepped closer, his nightcap sitting crooked on a nest of wild hair springing from the sides of his head. He leaned forward to examine her face. "Ain't you Miss Madison? What happened? You hurt?"

The answers to his questions froze in her mind. How would she explain? "I-I fell."

"You got no business being out here in the middle

of the night, ma'am." He looked around. "You alone? I thought I heard a man's voice."

"I was …"

His chest rumbled with a growl, and he tipped closer until a mere few inches separated her from his Roman nose. "Did some no-good, cowardly rogue run off and leave you to face the music alone?"

"Yes, but …" He misunderstood the situation, and her stumbling words didn't help. A clear explanation—along with her newfound courage and independence—deserted her with the speed of her attacker.

Concerned comments turned into a buzz of horrid accusations. Several shivering women pointed and whispered together. By sunset tomorrow, the gossip will have traveled miles. Her reputation will be tattered, her business ruined, and any chance of a future with Hugh Barnes made impossible.

Merry Christmas, Violet.

She clenched her fists and a spasm of pain shot up her left arm.

Movement across the street alerted her to the presence of someone among the bushes. Had her attacker returned? She squinted in an effort to distinguish the face of the man ready to stride toward the circle of neighbors. Hugh?

What was he doing here? How did he know?

With a slow, steady motion, she shook her head. He stopped. She repeated the signal, praying he didn't insist upon being heroic. He'd only make things worse for both of them, and she couldn't let him become embroiled in this fiasco. She released a breath as he slipped behind an evergreen.

"Is that Santa Claus, Mama?" The tiny girl tugged on her mother's coat.

"No, dear."

"Is she an angel?"

"Hush, Myrtle. The woman most certainly is no angel."

Violet covered her mouth to hold back a burst of hysterical laughter. Her whole future had just fallen apart, and she found the question of a small child the funniest, most bizarre thing she had heard all evening.

***

The branch of the evergreen in Hugh's grip snapped in two. Everything in him wanted to rush to Violet's aid, but she'd been right in stopping him. He didn't care about himself, but what little he could hear of the comments bandied about convinced him his sudden arrival would only confirm their suppositions.

Tell them, Violet. Tell them your secret.

The crowd broke up and drifted back to their homes, leaving Violet standing alone. She clutched her arm to her body and lumbered down the street to be swallowed whole by the darkness. Hugh ran after her. When he closed the distance between them, she spun and raised the stick.

"Violet, it's me."

89

She whispered, "What are you doing here?"

"I've been following you. I know all about The Yuletide Angel." He pointed to the walking stick. "Please, put the weapon down."

Violet eyed the stick as if she'd forgotten she held it. She opened her fingers, and it hit the ground with a *thump* and a bounce. "How did you—"

"We'll discuss it later. Right now, we need to get you home." He winced as she cradled her left arm in front of her. "Is it broken?"

"Sprained, I think."

"What happened?"

"Someone knocked me down."

His heart fell to his stomach as one more fear was realized. "You were attacked? By whom?"

"I didn't see his face. He ran off, but I smelled liquor."

Nearby, a dog barked. Hugh picked up the walking stick, then moved to the opposite side of her injured wrist and wrapped an arm around her shoulders. "Let's get you out of here before we attract more company."

She pressed close to him during the walk back to the Madison house. Once they arrived, he opened the door and ushered her inside the parlor. A puff of breath stuttered from her as he removed her coat.

Violet dropped onto the sofa in the middle of the room. She uttered no other sound as he lit the lamp on a table.

Hugh paced in front of the sofa. "Violet, let people know why you were out tonight and what happened.

They'll understand. They'll admire and praise you for your generosity."

"I don't want praise. Praise is for God alone." A flicker of bewilderment crossed her face and disappeared with a shake of her head. "Please go home before you wake Charles and Lila."

"What will you tell him? He's going to hear about what happened."

"I don't know. Even if I explained, I'm not sure anyone would believe me. The man grabbed the sacks before he ran off, so what proof is there?"

Other than Hugh admitting he'd skulked behind her each night?

"I'm not about to leave you to deal with your brother on your own." He knelt before her. "This whole mess is my fault. In hindsight, I wish I'd stepped forward when you faced that crowd tonight."

He'd promised himself—he'd promised God—that he would protect her as she went about her charitable work. He'd failed, and now she would suffer the consequences. "I should have stopped you the first time I saw you sneaking off in the night."

Her jaw dropped. "How long have you known?"

"Since the first Wednesday. I saw you from my window and have followed you each week, trying to keep you safe." Wry laughter rumbled in his chest. "Fine protector I am."

Footsteps pounded the stairs, and they both focused on the room's doorway. Hugh jumped up as the light from a lamp preceded Charles into the parlor. He glanced from one to the other of them. "What's going on? Violet, why aren't you in bed? And what are you doing here at this hour, Barnes?"

He appeared more dumbfounded than irate, but Hugh expected that to change once the shock wore off.

"Charles, what is it?" Lila hurried into the room, her braid bouncing over one shoulder. She stopped behind her husband with her hand at her throat. "Oh."

"Go back to bed, dear. I'll handle this."

Lila spotted Violet cradling her arm and rushed to the sofa. "You're hurt. Let me see." Even though her sister-in-law took great care in examining the wrist with tenderness, Violet sucked air through her teeth at the woman's touch. "It's swollen. I'll heat water for a compress."

After she left, Charles gained his wits. "I want the whole story and I want it right now."

Violet lowered her chin. "Hugh ... Mr. Barnes ..."

He placed himself between Violet and her brother. "It's good you're awake, Charles. I'd like to ask for your sister's hand in marriage."

***

Had she heard Hugh correctly? Marriage? Tears filled Violet's eyes. Tears of happiness. Tears of heartache. That sweet, noble man.

Charles faced Hugh, who stood with his back to Violet. Her brother's mouth compressed into a scowl.

"I'm asking for your permission to make Violet my wife, Charles."

She loved Hugh so much, too much to allow him to make such a sacrifice. "This isn't necessary. I appreciate what you're trying to do, but I won't marry you, not under these circumstances."

Charles crossed his arms over his dressing gown. "What circumstances? You're here in the middle of the night to ask my permission to marry my sister? You had occasion to do so earlier this evening. Why now? Just how did Violet injure her arm?"

She gasped. "Charles, he had nothing to do with it. I fell."

"Quiet, Violet. This discussion is between Mr. Barnes and me." Both men glared at one another. "Well?"

Oh, for pity's sake. She wouldn't sit here and let her brother think the worst of Hugh. And she couldn't let a scandal she caused ruin his future. "I was attacked, Charles."

Both men flinched at the simple statement. Hugh turned and offered her a smile that revealed his sympathy while her brother's mouth gaped. Charles settled next to her and gripped Violet's uninjured hand in his. "What do you mean you were attacked? By whom?"

"I-I leave the house in the middle of the night to deliver food to the poor. Tonight I sensed someone nearby. It scared me, so I ran. Unfortunately, I ran right into the man. He knocked me down and stole the food sacks."

 93

"You deliver food to the poor in the middle of the night?" Charles drew in a breath as comprehension dawned. "Are you claiming to be that Yuletide Angel person? No. Preposterous."

"It's true."

She sat motionless as he studied her face, presumably searching for falsehood. He turned to Hugh. "And what is your role in her clandestine activity? Surely you have one or you wouldn't be here."

Hugh glanced at her before saying, "Several weeks ago, I discovered Violet's ill-advised generosity."

Ill-advised generosity?

While the term stirred her ire, it stirred something else in her too, something more disturbing. Earlier, she had denied wanting praise. Praise was for God, she'd said. At the time, a little voice inside warned her to re-evaluate her motives, but she'd ignored it. In truth, no matter how much she denied it to herself, not hearing the typical tales of gratitude from those who received her gifts had annoyed her. When had her anonymous gift-giving changed from humble generosity to a puffed-up desire for appreciation?

Violet's shoulders drooped. *Please forgive me, Lord, for allowing my purpose to become pride.*

"I've been following her in an attempt to protect her from ruffians prowling the streets." Hugh's voice faded on the last few words.

"Yes, I see how well you did your job. And you expect me to trust you to protect my sister in marriage?"

Hadn't she recently bemoaned the idea of a man's protection? She wanted to look out for herself. She should be angry with both of them. Why then did the idea of Hugh's efforts not bother her? "Please stop, Charles."

"Are you in pain, dear?"

Violet slipped her hand from her brother's. "Only when it comes to my vanity. I owe you an apology, Hugh."

"Me? If anyone should apologize—"

She raised her good hand. "No. You've shown what a kind and considerate man you are by everything you've done for me. Even when you had no responsibility to tramp about in the cold, you laid aside your comfort to see to my safety. I'm the one who put us both in jeopardy. Now you've proposed to save my reputation. You're a gentleman, Hugh Barnes, and I lo … I admire you for it."

Hugh stepped closer. "Violet—"

"God blesses our giving when it's done from our hearts, but I allowed my method to turn into a matter of pride, just like those who sound a trumpet seeking the praise of others. Because of that pride, I've discredited myself and the Madison name."

Charles leaned back. "Discredited? How?"

Her chest tightened, but she refused to look away. "When I fell, my scream brought the neighbors from their homes. They misunderstood my reason for being out so late."

Her brother's face paled. "Did they see you too, Barnes?"

A muscle in Hugh's jaw jumped. "No."

"Thank goodness for that."

Lila carried a bowl of steaming water and a towel into the parlor. She stopped inside the room. Her glance leapt from one to another of its occupants before she continued to the sofa and wrapped Violet's wrist with a hot compress. "This will help the swelling, but you mustn't use the arm."

"Thank you, Lila."

The ring of the front door sounded. "What now?" Charles left the room and returned with Kit Barnes.

"What is it, Kit?"

"I'd ask you the same, Hugh, but it would be pointless." The younger man marched straight to his brother. "Can I speak with you? Privately."

"Can it wait?"

"No."

The two men stepped into the foyer. A moment later, Hugh said a quick good-bye and rushed out the door with Kit.

Violet's tears rose to the surface. He took with him his offer to protect her ... to marry her. And she was heartbroken.

CHAPTER ELEVEN

Violet rested her head along the sofa back. Hugh and Kit had been gone for almost an hour. She should go upstairs to bed—they all should—but despite her disappointment when he left, somehow she knew he'd return.

A few minutes later the doorbell sounded, and she sprang from her seat. Charles let in the men, along with Mitch Collinsworth and his sister. Their uncle lagged behind—hat in hand, hair tousled, and a lump like a unicorn's horn protruding from his forehead. Even from several feet away Wendell Collinsworth reeked of drink and wobbled on his feet.

"I'm glad you're awake." Hugh removed his hat and tossed it on a nearby chair. Excitement and intensity sprang from every motion. "Let's get this matter settled, darling."

Violet's heart tripped over the endearment. She longed to hear it over and over for the remainder of her life.

Charles wrinkled his nose as Mr. Collinsworth passed him. "So you brought children and a drunkard with you?"

Hugh placed a hand on the boy's shoulder. "Mitch came to my house earlier to find Kit and tell him his uncle had slipped out in the night."

Kit grunted. "An epidemic in this town."

Ignoring his brother's sarcasm, Hugh said, "The boy worried that Wendell's intent wasn't to go to the tavern this time, but to follow Miss Madison."

Violet glanced at the boy. "Me? Why?"

"I, uh …" Mitch shifted from one foot to the other. "I saw you the first time you delivered food to us."

"He was outside, looking for his uncle at the time."

Kit's statement rekindled Violet's fear. "I remember hearing the crack of a twig and thought someone watched me." Violet rolled her eyes. "I've had so many people attached to me I might as well have been the engine of a train."

Hugh chuckled. "He recognized Violet while visiting my store a few days later. Mitch told his uncle, and Wendell made him promise not to tell anyone else."

"If I'd a notion of what he planned to do, Miss Madison, I woulda never said nothin', especially after you was so nice when I stole the cookies."

"You stole cookies while at the store?" Hugh glanced at Mitch. "Anything else?"

"No, sir. I promised Miss Madison I wouldn't. But …"

Hugh grimaced as his gaze followed that of the boy's to his uncle. The latter looked away. "We'll deal with your activities at my store later, Collinsworth." He turned back to Violet. "Last Thursday Mitch woke up to discover the kitchen shelves filled with canned food. The boy is smart. It didn't take him long to figure out how it got there."

Outraged, Violet shook her finger at the uncle. "You stole the food I delivered to other needy people? How could you, Mr. Collinsworth?"

His shrug left him off-balance and he caught the parlor door frame to keep from falling.

Charles huffed. "What does this have to do with tonight and my sister's injury?"

Violet bit back the urge to tell her brother to clear the feathers from his tired brain.

"Let's let Wendell speak." Kit glanced behind him at the inebriated man.

Mr. Collinsworth squeezed the life from his hat with trembling hands. "I only wanted the food. But I musta made a noise, 'cause she got scared and took to runnin', only she run right into me. Then she had that stick and kept hittin' me with it." He pointed to his head. "Look here what she done."

Though Violet shook inside, she itched to grab the walking stick and give him another lump for good measure. Her own culpability and her sprained wrist were all that stopped her.

"Look at what *she* did?" Hugh's arms flapped. "Do you realize what you've done to this woman?"

"Hold up, Hugh. There's more, Mr. Madison." Kit scowled at Mr. Collinsworth. "Go ahead."

 99

The man ducked his head. "Well, I knocked her down so she'd stop hittin' me, then grabbed the sacks and run. I took 'em home and went back to the tavern."

Kit glanced at his brother. "I came for Hugh after I found Wendell there, fully inebriated, and spreading the identity of The Yuletide Angel to anyone who would listen."

"How dare you mention my sister's name in such a disgraceful place, Collinsworth!" Charles' voice rose with each syllable.

Violet turned away. She reached up her left sleeve and withdrew her handkerchief, then stuffed it back inside, realizing her inability to twist it with one hand.

Supporting her arm, she shuffled to the Christmas tree near the front window. The scents of cranberries and pine hung heavy in the room. She tilted her head back to view the angel at the top of the tree—the herald announcing the birth of the Christ-child.

God's angels sang of His glory. They did not seek glory for themselves. Like those messengers, she had not intended to broadcast her own deeds. She cringed at trumpeting her actions.

Now, she had no need to worry over doing so. Everyone in town would do it for her.

***

Hugh walked up behind Violet and placed his hands on her shoulders. "This isn't a bad thing, you know."

"Isn't it?"

He turned her to him and ached at witnessing the slack features and dull eyes. "Don't you see? Gossip travels faster than a thoroughbred through this town. It won't be long until everyone knows why you were out tonight. Who will criticize The Angel for doing what she believes God called her to do?"

"That's the problem, Hugh. I'm no angel. I believe God wanted me to provide food for those in need. He didn't say I was to traipse about in the middle of the night leaving it in secret. I realize now that it was my own idea, born from my timidity."

"Dearest …" From now on, he'd pamper her with sweet words just to see a rosy glow light her face. "Look at the joy and anticipation you've brought others. We've both heard the stories. People delighted in knowing you visited them more than they appreciated the food."

"But that doesn't mean it was given with the right spirit. I wasn't to take undue pleasure in their approval."

"When you had the opportunity to tell those people who you were tonight, you didn't take it. Why not?"

"Because I didn't want the pra—" She clamped her mouth shut.

"You can't deny you have a heart for the needy, Violet. You also can't deny that you're human, and as human beings, we all sin." He glanced at his brother who was busy handing sticks of candy to the children while their uncle slumped against a parlor wall, fast asleep. Hugh thanked God for showing him his lack of forgiveness when it came to Kit. "If we were perfect, would there be a need to celebrate the coming of Jesus, the One who paid the price for those sins?"

She flashed one of those astounding smiles. "No, there wouldn't."

Hugh's strong exhale echoed in a room that had grown quiet as everyone watched them. The skin along his hairline sprouted tiny beads of sweat when Charles nodded. It was all the permission he needed.

"Come on." Hugh helped Violet into her coat, careful of her injured wrist.

"Where are we going?"

"Where we can talk." He glanced over his shoulder at the crowded parlor. "Alone."

He led her through the kitchen, out the back door, and into the crispness of the morning chill. Facing his house, the two of them sat side-by-side on the porch steps, their arms touching. Dawn brightened the sky with glorious blends of orange and red until the rising sun lit the day with its golden light. For the rest of his life, he'd crave the warmth that washed through him while in the presence of Violet—his everlasting love.

"Mr. Collinsworth is not a proper parent, but what will happen to the children?" Her low-spoken question broke the comfortable silence between them.

"Kit's had experience with such circumstances and will see to their welfare. They'll be fine."

"Your brother has become a good man."

"I know."

She angled her knees toward him. "Merry Christmas, Hugh."

"Merry Christmas, Violet."

He clasped her hand and slid his thumb back and forth across the cool, smooth skin, then chuckled at her sigh of contentment.

"I meant what I said to Charles." He pointed toward his home. "This summer, I want to sit in wicker chairs on the front porch of that house with you and watch the sun set in the evening, then see it rise from the second-story window at dawn. Every day, I want to sail with you on that ship that leads us through years of adventure."

"Y-you still want to marry me?" Spots of morning light reflected in the glassy sheen of her eyes.

"More than anything. I want to love and protect you for the rest of our lives."

Her chin dipped. "Even though I've been a pride-filled fool?"

"Oh, my beautiful Violet, don't talk about yourself like that." He lifted her chin so she could witness the depth of his love for her. "No matter what, you have my heart. You always will."

"My family's idea of protection meant discouraging me from experiencing life. By helping me start my bakery business and not stopping my generosity—however ill-advised—you've allowed me that freedom. Thank you, Hugh."

She tilted her head at an enticing angle and leaned into him. Hugh's palms grew moist, and the pulse in his neck throbbed when she paused, so close the warmth of their breaths mingled. She gently pressed her soft lips to his.

 103

As Violet drew back, her eyes widened in surprise, and then softened into an expression of love so undeniable Hugh needed to remind himself to breathe.

He pulled in a deep lungful of air and released it, then cupped the side of her face in his hand. "How bold you've become, Miss Madison. Might I suggest we marry soon before I require protection from you?"

She rested her head on his shoulder. "I can't think of a better idea, Mr. Barnes."

Careful of her wrist, he wrapped her in his arms … right where The Yuletide Angel belonged.

22890922R00066

Made in the USA
Middletown, DE
14 December 2018